THE VIRTUAL LIBRARIAN

Other Rockwell Books

Ted: *Arms Control Agreements: Designs for Verification* (co-author), Johns Hopkins Press (1968), used in connection with US-USSR talks at the White House.
Ted: *The Rickover Effect: How One Man Made a Difference,* Naval Institute Press (1992); Chinese language edition (1994); John Wiley paperback (1995). Authors Guild Edition, via iUniverse Excerpted in *Reader's Digest,* domestic and foreign.
Ted: *Creating the New World: Stories & Images from the Dawn of the Atomic Age,* AuthorHouse (2003), won first-place in the Science category of the ninth annual Independent Publishers Book Awards. Also acclaimed Book of the Year (non-fiction) in the JADA Press Annual Book Award Competition, and Book of the Month by the Manhattan Project Heritage Preservation Association.
Bob: *VRML-97: Der Neue Standard fuer Interactive 3D-Welten im World Wide Web* (co-author), Addison-Wesley (1998).
Teed: *Neither Brain nor Ghost: A Nondualist Alternative to the Mind-Brain Identity Theory,* MIT Press (2005)

Some Rockwell Articles

Ted: "Frontier Life Among the Atom Splitters," *Saturday Evening Post,* Dec 1, 1945.
Ted: "Bred For Fury," *True,* Jul 1946 (First color stroboflash photos of fighting cocks in action).
Ted: "Report of Panel on Science and Unexplained Phenomena," *American Society for Information Science,* U.S. Bicentennial Conference, Apr 12–14, 1976 (Chaired by Robert Kennedy, Sr.).
Ted: "Parapsychology and the Integrity of Science," *Washington Post* (Sunday OpEd), Page D8, Aug 26, 1979.
Ted: "How Should Science Handle the 'Unbelievable'?" Testimony and report to Congressional Office of Technology Assessment, Oct 30, 1988.
Bob: "An Infrastructure for Social Software," *IEEE Spectrum* (Mar 1997).
Bob: "Infrastructure and Architecture for Cyberspace Communities," *Computer Graphics—ACM SIGGRAPH* (Nov 1997).
Bob: "Getting Together in Cyberspace," *VRML 95 Symposium, SDSC* (Dec 1995).
Bob: "Software Development is a Communication Process," *Proc. 2nd European Workshop on the Software Process,* Trondheim, Norway (Sep 1992).
Bob: "Why Life-Cycle Processes (Don't) Work," *Proc. 4th International Software Process Workshop, IEEE Press* (1992).
Teed: "God, Freedom & Darwin: Where Science Stops and Theology Begins," Workshop Reference Manual (2007)

Juanita: "Toward a Semiotic of Theatre," In *The Leviathan,* Colorado Springs (1980)
Juanita: Libretto for James Sellars's opera, *The World is Round* (based on Gertrude Stein's book). Hog River Music (1994).
Ted, Bob,& Teed: "Irrational Rationalists," *Jour. Amer. Soc. Psychical Research,* 72, 23–34, (Jan 1978). Reprinted in *The Battlefield of Psi* (Japanese language anthology, 1987).
Ted & Teed: Chapter in *Der Wissenschaftler und das Irrationale,* Hans Peter Duerr (Editor), Frankfurt, Syndikat (1981).
Ted & Teed: "Heresy, Excommunication, and Other Weeds in the Garden of Science," *New Realities* (Dec 1981).
Ted & Teed: "Demarcation Between Science & Pseudoscience" (Book Review) *J.Am.Soc.Psch.Res* (Jan 1986).
Ted & Teed: "Frames of Meaning: The Social Construction of Extraordinary Science" (Book Review), *Theta* 11 (1983).
Ted & Teed: "Margins of Reality: The Role of Consciousness in the Physical World" (Book Review), *Theta* 10 (1982)

The Virtual Librarian

A Tale of Alternative Realities

Ted & Bob Rockwell

Magnificently Illustrated by Thomas Chalkley

Computer Drawings Artfully Crafted by Nevin Hoke

iUniverse, Inc.
New York Lincoln Shanghai

THE VIRTUAL LIBRARIAN
A TALE OF ALTERNATIVE REALITIES

Copyright © 2008 by Theodore Rockwell

All rights reserved. No part of this book may be used or reproduced by any means, graphic, electronic, or mechanical, including photocopying, recording, taping or by any information storage retrieval system without the written permission of the publisher except in the case of brief quotations embodied in critical articles and reviews.

iUniverse books may be ordered through booksellers or by contacting:

iUniverse
2021 Pine Lake Road, Suite 100
Lincoln, NE 68512
www.iuniverse.com
1-800-Authors (1-800-288-4677)

Because of the dynamic nature of the Internet, any Web addresses or links contained in this book may have changed since publication and may no longer be valid.

Certain characters in this work are historical figures, and certain events portrayed did take place. However, this is a work of fiction. All of the other characters, names, and events as well as all places, incidents, organizations, and dialogue in this novel are either the products of the author's imagination or are used fictitiously.

ISBN: 978-0-595-47390-8 (pbk)
ISBN: 978-0-595-71071-3 (cloth)
ISBN: 978-0-595-91668-9 (ebk)

Printed in the United States of America

THE STORY

	Acknowledgements ix	
	Preface xi	
Mon., April 9, 20??	Scene 1:	The Demo 1
Mon., April 9	Scene 2:	Quality Time 7
Tues., April 10	Scene 3:	The Briefing 15
Tues., April 10	Scene 4:	The Dream 25
Fri., April 13	Scene 5:	The World of Psi 29
Wed., April 18	Scene 6:	It's Gonna Evolve! 35
Fri., April 20	Scene 7:	Kim 41
Mon., April 30	Scene 8:	Mind Control 45
Tues., May 1	Scene 9:	"Look At It Go!" 51
Sun., May 20	Scene 10:	Silva Mind Control 55
Tues., May 22	Scene 11:	Getting to Know Lib 59
Fri., May 25	Scene 12:	Computers and the PEAR Lab 63
Sat., May 26	Scene 13:	Out of Control 71
Sat., May 26	Scene 14:	Spindrift and the New World Order 75
Tues., May 29	Scene 15:	Psych Attack? 83
Wed., May 30	Scene 16:	Summit Meeting 87
Thurs., May 31	Scene 17:	CyberTek 89
Sat., June 2	Scene 18:	Witch Hunt 95
Mon., June 4	Scene 19:	Power to the People 99
Tues., June 5	Scene 20:	Go Get 'Em 103
Sat., June 9	Scene 21:	A Delphic Circle 107
Mon., June 11	Scene 22:	The Post-Mortem 113
Tues., June 12	Scene 23:	Complexity 117
Sat., June 16	Scene 24:	Psychic Shrinks 127
Tues., June 19	Scene 25:	A Real Shrink 133
Fri., June 22	Scene 26:	She 135
Mon., June 25	Scene 27:	The Lobotomy 139
Wed., June 27	Scene 28:	The Zombie 141
Fri., June 29	Scene 29:	Awakenings 147
March, 1997	Epilogue:	The Potential Wonders of Virtual Worlds . . 157

ACKNOWLEDGEMENTS

No book is the product of just its authors, and this one is no exception. Luckily, illustrator **Tom Chalkley** (www.TomChalk.com) seemed to know the characters in this novel as well as I did and was able to faithfully describe in pen and ink the figures I created with words. Designing computer figures is no less an art than illustration, and draftsman/designer **Nevin Hoke** (nhoke@mpr.com) was able to create exactly what was needed.

Since I am new to the craft of fiction-writing, I benefited immensely from advice and assistance of novelists **Sam Schreiner**, **Gwyneth Cravens**, and **Jack Laflin**. The editing skills and storytelling instincts of **Connie Buchanan** and **Paisley Griffin** were also critically helpful during several stages in the years-long writing process. iUniverse Publishing Services Associate **Melissa Rose** was crucial in steering this manuscript through the rocky shoals toward bookhood. I also owe thanks to editor **Alison Cherry** and the anonymous **iUniverse editors** whose editorial evaluation report helped clear up some remaining flaws and errors. And to the good people of **TheSLAgency.com**, who taught me a few things about carrying out promotion in a virtual world. I owe thanks to my children, **Teed**, **Larry**, and **Juanita**, who brought their unique skills and insights to this book. And of course, thanks to my deceased, first-born son, **Bob**, who started it all.

To my long-suffering wife, **Mary Rockwell**, from whom I was diverted as she tried to recover from a severe stroke, I offer my apologies, love, and appreciation.

Ted Rockwell

PREFACE:
AN OTHERWORLDLY VISION

I started writing this story in 1995, inspired by long, passionate, late-night discussions with my first-born, Bob. He was a zealous pioneer, preaching the importance of understanding the role that information played in modern life and of developing techniques for computers to implement that role. By 1975, he was already developing new tools to put complex, numerical information into visual formats for practical use. Later, as a PhD in cultural anthropology, he saw the possibilities that might stem from 3-D, virtual communities, and as "Preacher," he became a leader in that new field.

In April of 1998, Bob died suddenly and unexpectedly, and I put the manuscript away. However, though I missed his input sorely, I later decided to finish what we had started with the help of my other grown children Teed, Larry, and Juanita. It seemed fitting to include as an epilogue a little story that Bob wrote in 1996; in March of 1997, this story was also incorporated into a major article for the internationally respected technical journal *Spectrum*, published by the Institute of Electrical and Electronic Engineers. The story demonstrated his vision of how virtual reality might become a part of the all-too-physical reality that surrounds us today.

All of the active characters in this book are fictional. Their adventures are also fictional. But I've mentioned a number of real people who have done research relevant to the plot. All of the researchers and research findings are real. The engineering businesses I describe are based on firms and practices I have observed firsthand. This book is like a historical novel in which the kings, battles, plagues, and treaties are all historical facts and the fictional story gives us a way to visit a very different world that we could not otherwise access.

I describe only two real people, who briefly interact with the story's characters: the late Christian Science healer Bruce Klingbeil, and the former Princeton Dean of Engineering, Professor Robert Jahn. Their dialogue includes only the sorts of ideas about which they have written and spoken. I do not speculate about what they might say about things they never actually discussed.

The strange psychic experiences in the book are taken from events I have personally experienced. I have had audiences with yogis, swamis, lamas, sufis, indigenous healers, an exorcist, and the Dalai Lama at his government-in-exile in Dharamsala. I have done a firewalk, and I have taken advanced Silva Mind Control under Jose Silva. I've done Archaeus, Noetics, Neuro-Linguistic Programming, ChiOps, est, and HemiSynch and have taken other mind-expanding courses. I've interacted with many of the New Age pioneers, and consulted with J. B. Rhine during the twelve years that I was the designated representative of the Parapsychological Association to the American Association for the Advancement of Science—the "representative of the Kooks to the Squares." The psychics in the story are based on real people I know and things I have seen them do.

I have also dabbled in some of the computer techniques discussed in the book; I started programming in the 1950s, penciling in ones and zeros and working with large stacks of perforated IBM cards. I have typed questions to Apple's Rogerian psychoanalyst on my 1979 Apple II+ computer and heard him respond helpfully in his Viennese accent. I have explored some of the "bleeding edge" techniques, played virtual golf, and operated a "wearable computer."

So in a sense, nearly everything in this story is "true" and "real." All the research findings I have cited are real. In the 1990s, the dream that virtual worlds would become part of the common experience was ahead of the available technical resources. But now the technology is catching up, and the burgeoning popularity of Lib's virtual world is discussed in the major cover story on "Second Earth" in the July/August, 2007 issue of *Technology Review.*

This story is pure fiction. But you may hear such stories on tomorrow's newscasts.

Ted Rockwell

KEITH

MONDAY, APRIL 9: INFOPOWER'S DEVELOPMENT LAB

For the past couple of weeks, people had been signing up for sneak previews of the new Virtual Reality Library, and Keith Robertson decided to drop by the lab at lunchtime to see if he could squeeze in a demo for himself. At forty-five, Keith was a senior engineer on special assignment at InfoPower, a leading firm in the fast-growing world of information technology. He had heard so much hype about the Library that he was eager to experience it for himself. He smiled as he realized that he had bought into the buzz—you don't *see* the Library, you *experience* it.

As he rounded the corner and headed toward the lab, he could immediately see that he was not going to get an unscheduled demo today. A carnival atmosphere emanated from the crowd milling around the entrance to the lab. Kim Lee, the sharp, young, Korean computer engineer, who had graduated first in his class at CalTech and whose English was now as full of technical slang and American jive as any native son, was taking extreme pleasure in showing off his creation. Kim was slim, cool, and fast-talking, but not noisy. He could shift his glib chatter seamlessly into professorial tutorial mode when needed, and he seemed to delight in that role.

Ginger, the slim, red-haired analyst from Engineering, was sitting in the easy chair in front of the control console. She was wearing a helmet that came down over her eyes and ears. A mass of wires was gathered neatly into a bundle at the back and fed into the side of the control box. Ginger was clawing the air wildly and squealing with excitement. The whole crowd was enjoying her experience, and Keith had the feeling she was probably getting a longer "ride" than some of her more taciturn and less attractive colleagues.

"We experimented with rollers you could walk on," explained Kim to the crowd, "and it made for a very real experience. We even programmed in the sound of footsteps—soft soles for the men, high heels for the ladies." He acknowledged the murmurs of approval. "But who wants to do all your research standing up? So we have this comfortable chair for you to sit in. When you want to move forward, you lean forward slightly, and you glide in the direction you want to go. The further you lean, the faster you move."

"How do you produce that spectacular 3-D effect?" asked one of the engineers.

"We looked at several ways to do that," said Kim. "There's a setup that's commercially available for your desktop PC that can create a 3-D effect on your monitor ingeniously. Left- and right-eye images are projected alternately on the screen at a fast rate, and special glasses alternately black out one eye and then the other in sync with the screen. There are other systems in which the image is projected onto a sort of visor on your helmet. We decided it was easiest to just have two separate, tiny viewing screens—one in front of each eye. One shows the view from the left eyeball, the other from the right. It was sort of a pain to set up and program, but once you do it, it's done. You don't have to keep tinkering with that part of it. And … it's very convincing, as you've seen."

Ginger suddenly stopped squealing and said in a queasy voice, "I want to get off." One of the technicians stepped forward and took off her wired helmet and her sensory-input gloves. She looked pretty woozy.

"Tell us what you were doing," said Kim. "There's an important lesson here for everybody."

"I was sorta skating down the hall and maybe swirling around a little, like a ballerina. It felt great! And then, when you showed me the globe, I sorta made like I was a bird. I swooped down on it and skimmed along the rivers and over the mountains, and—Uh-oh. I don't feel so good." And she got up and stumbled unsteadily toward the restroom, accompanied by two sympathetic and curious colleagues.

"I couldn't have made the point any clearer myself," said Kim. "You can get motion sickness from virtual motion. Does anybody need any further clarification on this point?" No one did.

The crowd raised further questions about locating and handling information. "You can hold virtual reports in your hands and make notes in the margins," said Kim. "You can save the trail by which you got to a particular set of reports so that you can go back there. You can call up the full texts of any references in the bibliographies and footnotes. You can go tooling off down any side trails that interest you and come safely back whenever you want. Say you're reading about some process, and you see that somebody built a rig somewhere that you could test it on. You can follow that trail, get pictures of the equipment, call up the relevant patents. For key personnel, you can call up pictures, biographies, speeches, papers. As appropriate, these pictures may be in color or even move. You can hear speeches and see the visuals as the speakers point to them."

"But you can only get out what somebody has already put into the system," objected one of the older engineers—he was maybe thirty-five.

"Right! That's why it's so essential that you guys give us everything you've got that may be useful to somebody some day. But most of the technical stuff, like scientific reports in the public literature—journals, magazine articles, speeches, and the authors' biographical info—that's already on the Net somewhere, and we can simply retrieve it."

A slew of questions followed, and Keith listened, increasingly impressed. It was clear that this new toy was not going to suffer from neglect. Kim interrupted his reverie. "C'mon, Keith. There's always room to accommodate the big shots." He waved off Keith's protests.

Keith was at an awkward place in the company hierarchy. He spent most of his time with the techies, who didn't even own ties or jackets and couldn't care less about what happened in the front offices so long as they got their annual raises and bonuses. But Keith was called up to the front two or three times a week, and sometimes he had to talk with characters in dark suits, white shirts, and power ties. He had to be accepted in both worlds, though he often felt a little out of place in each. He always wore a jacket and a tie to work, but as soon as he got there, he loosened his tie and hung the jacket behind his door, ready if he needed it. He wore comfortable, padded, hush-puppy-style shoes. They were black and could pass for dress shoes if he wore them with a jacket.

Kim apparently didn't concern himself with such things. His place in this environment would still be secure if he wore purple tights. He pulled Keith by the arm toward the chair. Keith slipped on the wired gloves. "Tell me about these," he said. He knew most of the answers, but he was acting as straight man for Kim's tutorial.

"They're more or less standard data gloves," said Kim. "We bought 'em commercially."

"But, I mean, what do they do?" Most of the technies knew some general facts about data gloves, but Keith wasn't taking anything for granted here. He had learned not to assume that they—or he—knew the answers to important questions.

"These gloves are your tactile interface with our virtual world," explained Kim. "When you reach out to pick up a book, you'll feel it in your fingers when you grab it. If you push on a wall, it will resist. It's an important aspect of making you really believe—not just in your rational brain—that you are there in that world. You're not just observing it from outside. Believe me, Keith, it makes a difference."

"Hey, I believe!" said Keith with mock-evangelical fervor. "But I want to understand, too." He put on the helmet, adjusted it until the image was clear, and suddenly shouted, "Wow! Look at that!"

"Tell us what you see," instructed Kim.

Keith was silent for a minute, overcome by what he saw and felt. The colors were bright but not garish. The color scheme was soft and mellow—gold and brown and cream with soft green trim. There were no light bulbs anywhere, but everything seemed to glow from within. There were highlights but only suggestions of shadows. The 3-D effects were incredible. He was really there.

He started to talk a couple of times, broke into sheepish giggles, and then said softly, "It's like a dream, just like a dream. You know how toward the end of a particularly vivid dream, you feel way in the back of your mind somewhere that it seems more real than reality? You feel like when you wake up, the real world is going to seem pale and insubstantial by comparison."

Keith was in a huge library filled with aisles and hallways that seemed to go on infinitely in every direction. But there were no tables or chairs, no reading lamps, no drinking fountains, no magazine racks—nothing of that sort. And there were no people, except for one librarian. There were many more technical journals, papers, and various sorts of files than there were books. And there was a bulletin board with various notices on it. As Keith leaned forward just a little to look at the bulletin board, he glided right up to it without making any effort. He just drifted closer until he was within easy reading distance.

There were no dog-eared magazines or books shelved upside down, as you might see in an ordinary library. There was no graffiti and no litter on the floor. It seemed like some sort of utopian dream. Keith looked down one of the aisles and started drifting down it. Of course, he didn't know where anything was, so he turned to the librarian, who always seemed to be at his side when he needed her.

"Not your stereotypical, old-maid librarian, eh?" Kim's voice broke in.

"No, no," replied Keith with enthusiasm. "Lovely ... lovely."

"Keith," asked Kim, "do you see that big push-button on the bulletin board that looks like a globe with the continents all colored in? See it? It should be right in front of you, unless you've taken off down a corridor."

"Yeah, wait a minute. I'll get back there," said Keith. "Okay, it's right here. Should I push it?"

"Go ahead. A great big globe will appear, suspended a comfortable distance from your face. You can turn it around with your hands and point to any spot on it, and you'll zoom in on that spot."

Keith found himself diving like a hawk toward the state of New York. The mountains and rivers and cities, all rendered in bright, cloudless detail, were as realistic as if he were looking down from a helicopter. But the state boundaries were drawn in with thin, bright yellow lines, and the cities and highways were marked and labeled. He continued to zoom down toward a particular intersection he knew in Brooklyn. "Uh-oh," he said aloud. "I'm beginning to understand what happened to Ginger. I'm going to start zooming a little more sedately."

"That mapping capability," said Kim, "was actually commercially available. Of course, it's not completely filled in throughoutAsia or Africa, but every block of every street in America is there. You can come right down to our block here. You can also find any business or residential telephone number in the U.S. That capability was also commercially available. We're just puttin' a lot of stuff together."

"So it's not just a plaything."

"No way. Its main function, of course, is to find information that most companies keep in file cabinets and desk drawers. How do you find a critical document that one of your buddies has stuffed into the back of his desk? If it's in the electronic system, you can find it by title, by author, by company, by subject matter, by keyword, by date …"

"We had all that before," said Keith, "when we set up our stuff in digital format a couple of years ago. Does this virtual reality library really help us do our work better? Or is it just an excuse to play games with sexy librarians?"

"Look," said Kim a little defensively. He had apparently been kidded about the librarian before. "If you're going to create a librarian from scratch, why make an ugly one? It's like the library itself. We could've made it look beaten up and dirty, but why? Anyway, yes; it does make it easier to find information, and that's our bread and butter. Will it really pay its way? Who knows? But I'm sure gonna give it my best shot. I admire the guts of the management, pouring serious money into something this iffy."

Keith finessed that one. IP's board had not committed to finish this project, nor to keep him on indefinitely. He felt it was *his* neck on the line. His and Kim's.

"Let's test this thing. What do I do first?"

"Just act like you're talking to a real librarian. Ask for something."

Keith was always concerned about asking questions in the right way so that machines could handle them properly. Kim was just the opposite. Keith marveled at how he treated the Librarian like an intelligent child: no baby talk, no questions barred. He wanted her to learn to deal with the real world effectively and without help. Keith typed in, **I need some information.**

"How may I help you?" a pleasant, female voice asked over the loudspeaker. Her voice sounded natural and colloquial, which wasn't surprising—it was playing from a pre-recorded disc that the software had selected for this situation. The pretty face of the Librarian was smiling at him from the tiny screens. *So far, so good,* thought Keith. He hesitated, trying to think of a good test. Unlike a human librarian, the Librarian gave no sign of impatience.

Do you have any information on cobalt? I'd like to know the specific heat of cobalt. Pure cobalt. Not an alloy, Keith typed.

"Do you want a report on cobalt?" asked the loudspeaker. "Do you want a report on specific heat?"

Yes. Get me a report on cobalt.

"I have 43,786 reports with the word 'cobalt' in the title. I have 213,418 reports with the word 'cobalt' in the body of the text. Can you be more specific?"

"This is just a slow way to use Google," muttered Keith. **I need 'cobalt' and 'properties' in the title.**

"I have 138 reports with the word 'cobalt' in the title and also with the word 'properties' in the title."

How about adding "specific heat" in the body?

"Do you want reports with the word 'cobalt' and also the word 'properties' in the title and with the phrase 'specific heat' in the body of the text? If that is correct, please enter 'correct' or 'yes.' I have eighty-four reports that meet those criteria. Would you like to see the first five, ranked by recency of publication?"

"Recency?" asked Keith, to no one in particular. "These programs sure aren't being written by English teachers."

Yes. He didn't want to get into a further discussion with the Librarian, but she wasn't through yet. "I assume you want only reports in English. Is that correct?"

Yes.

"For future requests, unless you specify otherwise, do you want me to limit your information to that in English only? Please enter 'yes' or 'no,' and I will not have to ask this question again."

Keith shut off the machine in disgust. "Kim, we've got to do a lot better than this. The pretty graphics won't compensate for this kind of performance. I thought we were a lot further along."

Kim responded, somewhat defensively, "Yeah, I know. I could have opted for quicker and dirtier graphics and other support structures, but then we'd forever be going back to redo it. We've got the basic structure now, and it's pretty damn good. Now we have to start working on performance."

Keith was only half listening. He was trying to figure out whether the time and money he had been allotted could possibly do the job. The knot in his stomach was getting bigger and tighter.

MONDAY, APRIL 9: THE ROBERTSONS'S HOME

Joan Robertson was about Keith's age. She was pretty but not cute. She didn't always have time to keep her straight, brown hair fixed as nicely as she would like. She had a good eye for style and an excellent sense of what colors looked best on her, so she didn't have to spend a lot of money on her clothes. But the worry lines on her face were more prominent than you'd expect in someone her age, and her friends were sometimes startled when she responded to a casual remark of Keith's with more sarcasm and venom than seemed necessary.

She had been a technical librarian and then an executive secretary, so she partially understood what her husband and his company were doing. She wasn't hesitant about speaking her mind, and tonight she was doing just that. Keith had been breathlessly telling her about his new toy, and she had to cut in.

"Whoa! Hold your horses! You've been talking non-stop since you came in, and I don't think you've used one complete sentence yet. I'm confused."

"What don't you get, honey?"

"The big picture. Start at the beginning. What's virtual about this library, and who's Lib?"

"Well, the whole thing is virtual. I mean, this library has shelves and books and a librarian named Lib, but they're not made out of solid material. They exist only on a computer."

"That's what I don't get. Is it a hologram? Do you go into a Holodeck, like on Star Trek?"

"No, no. Oh, brother!" He paused. "You know those shoot-'em-up computer games you see in movie lobbies? They used to call them arcade games. There are bad guys and trees and so forth, but they only exist on the computer screen."

"Yeah," said Joan dubiously.

"Actually, it's more like a computer game like *Myst*, where you go down a long path through the forest. And you come to a castle. And inside the castle, there's a locked door. And you find a key. You can actually pick up the key and stick it in the lock, and the door opens. And all of this happens on the computer screen. It's a virtual world, not a real one."

"Yeah, but what's that got to do with a library?"

"Well, IP's virtual world has a virtual librarian. You see her on the screen. And you can talk with her. And she can answer questions and go get books and reports for you."

"So all you guys just crowd around a TV screen?"

"No, there's no big screen. Only one person can visit the library at a time. Well, we'll make more access chairs later. You sit in an easy chair, and there's a little screen right in front of each eyeball and stereo speakers alongside each ear. So there's a dramatic 3-D sense. You feel like you're really right there."

"Is this picture of a librarian just lip-synching while some guy behind a curtain is feeding her answers? What's the point of that?"

"No, that's the point of the program. There is no little man answering questions. The software creates the answers."

"How can that be? How can software make up answers? That sounds like magic."

"It sure does. And that's what makes it all so wonderful. But it's not that hard to do. Look, you've called an airline to find out whether a plane is late, right?"

"Yes, but—"

"You're not talking to a person when you do that. You're talking to software."

"But it doesn't sound like a machine. He doesn't talk in a monotone. It sounds very natural. I guess I never thought much about it. You're telling me I'm talking to a machine? There's nobody actually there? That's spooky."

"Yeah. Or like the woman talking to you from the GPS navigator in the car. There's no human backing her up, either." Keith looked down at his notes from the demo. "Hey, there was a software program called Eliza in 1966 that answered questions. It recognized only thirty-eight keywords and could draw on 112 canned responses, thirty-eight of which it constructed from what the user said. Even that was very convincing. If they could do that with programs that ran only a few hundred lines, think of what we can do today with millions of lines and gigabytes of memory and blinding speed. There's no limit, really."

This whole conversation had started when Keith walked into the house and interrupted an argument between Joan and their two kids. Eight-year-old Bud and his older sister Karen had been waiting with increasing impatience to get back to the argument. Now they both burst in, demanding to be heard.

"O-*kay*," said Joan. "Just a minute ... Keith, I've got enough information to hold me for a while. Let me settle this argument now."

Keith had enough sense to retreat from the battleground, and he went to the kitchen to get a beer. In the brief span of time he was gone, a full-scale argument developed. He listened for a moment as the volume built up, and then he had an idea. He headed back to the living room.

"Hey, this discussion isn't getting anywhere," he announced cheerfully. "How about you kids come with me, and we'll do something fun while Mommy fixes dinner. You want to eat tonight, don't you?"

Joan was glad for the interruption, but this wasn't an issue she could just drop. "They want to go over to the Rec Center for that talent show tomorrow, and I just can't take them. I have to get ready for the Den Meeting, or I'll have fifteen Cub Scouts at my throat."

"But we want to walk there," said Bud. "We've got a map, and it's not very far. What's the good of being a Cub Scout if you can't even take a little hike like that?"

Keith turned to Joan, who said, "It's way over toward Silver Spring. They don't know their way around over there. I can't just turn them loose. They might get lost."

"No, we won't!" shouted both kids at once.

Keith was ready for that one. "Let me have 'em for a little while, honey. I think I've got an answer. I've been meaning to talk with them about this anyway. We're going to work out something neat. Trust me—we'll check it out with you before anything happens. I get some quality time with the kids, and you get a few moments of peace. Deal?"

He gave her his best confident smile, and Joan knew she'd welcome the break. "Okay, but I get veto power over whatever you characters dream up." She turned and walked toward the kitchen, and the children ran to grab Daddy's hands as they walked out toward the street.

"What we need here is a GPS," said Keith. "Do you guys know what that is?" Eyes wide and faces solemn, they shook their heads.

"It stands for Geographic Position Sensor. It's an amazing little gadget. You can hold it in your hand like that little palm-top computer you've seen me use." Keith never talked down to his children—he treated them as he would treat an intelligent, foreign colleague who was uninformed about certain local facts and terminology.

"This gadget sends a little radio signal up to several satellites in orbit and measures exactly how long it takes for the signal to get to the satellite and back again. That tells you how far you are from each of those satellites. And look." Keith marked the ground with a stick to demonstrate his point. "Here's one satellite, and here's another. And you know you're this far from the first one and this far from the second one..." Keith drew an arc to the first satellite, using the first bump on the stick as a measuring stick, then drew a second arc to the second satellite.

"See how these two arcs cross each other? There's only one place that's the right distance from both. So that's where you are! How about that? Pretty neat, eh?"

He radiated excitement, and the kids began to get excited too. But Bud wasn't satisfied yet. "But you said 'several satellites.' How come? Why not just two?"

"Good question, Bud! You guys are really thinking. The extra ones are just to be sure. You know, in case some of the signals are a little weak. It's just for extra safety. Hey, if your pants fit and you button them up right, you probably don't need a belt. But the belt gives you extra safety, right?"

"Are you going to get us one of those gadgets, Daddy?" asked Karen incredulously.

"That would be pretty cool, wouldn't it?" agreed Keith. "But we'd need one for each of us, and they're pretty expensive. One of these days, I guess everyone will have one. But let me show you how you can do just as well without one. If you listen carefully, I'll show you how you can never get lost, and the only gadget you'll need is your head. You just have to remember to keep it turned on. Even the GPS doesn't work if it's turned off, and you can get lost if you turn your heads off. Are you both turned on?" They nodded vigorously. "The one thing you have to know is our address. What's our address?"

Joan had drilled that into them, and they were quick to reply. "4317 Chestnut Street."

"Right. Now, how did they pick that number? Did we just call up and ask for a number and get that one?"

The kids squirmed a little and looked puzzled. So Keith walked them up to the next house and pointed to the address. "4319," they both read dutifully.

"But where's 4318?" asked Keith.

"Across the street," said Karen.

"Right. So what's Mrs. Holmes's address?" asked Keith, pointing to the next house up the street.

"4321," said Karen after a brief hesitation. Bud nodded in agreement. "They're all odd numbers."

"Which side of the street has the odd numbers? North? South? East?" That stumped them for a minute. "Where do we see the pretty sunsets?"

"Over there," Karen and Bud replied.

"So what direction is that? Where does the sun set?"

"In the west."

"Okay. Now picture a big map of the U.S. stretched out before us on the ground. We're standing on Mexico and looking across the U.S. to Canada. Which direction are we looking?"

"North," they agreed.

"And where is the Atlantic Ocean? And where are the Rocky Mountains?"

They quickly figured that out, and Keith finally made his point. "So whenever you see odd numbers, you know you're looking north; east is on your right side, and west is on your left. Just picture that big map at your feet. Okay so far?"

Bud was smiling broadly, but Karen asked, "But Daddy, what about those streets going the other way? Some of them have odd numbers, and they're not north."

"Right. You guys are great! That's the next step. So far, you know two things: on streets going east and west, like our street, the numbers begin with forty-three, and they get bigger as you go west—right? So if you see a house with the number 4617, which way do you go to get home?"

They got that, but Karen still wasn't satisfied. "What about those other streets?"

"Let's go look at one," said Keith, taking her hand. They walked down to the crossroad. The house number was 7144. The next one south was 7142. "So now you know the other thing you need to know. North-south streets around here begin with seventy-one. So if you see an address like 6900, you know you are on a north-south street. Which way do you have to go to get home?"

"You have to go toward 7144. But which way is that?" asked Karen.

"It doesn't matter," Bud blurted out. "You just go the way that makes the numbers bigger."

"Exactly," said Keith. "And we just found out that that's north, didn't we? Do you know why these numbers are so high? Where do they all start? Is there a number one somewhere? Let's go back to the car, and I'll show you on the map."

He showed them that the U.S. Capitol was the zero point, and so they could tell that their home was seventy-one blocks north of the capitol and forty-three blocks west.

"Does Mommy know all this stuff?" asked Bud.

Keith looked at his watch. He'd given Joan enough time—she could handle them now. "Why don't you guys go in and tell her what you know about how not to get lost. We can even go and practice a little before you walk to the Rec Center, if Mommy thinks you should. But I'll bet she'll be amazed at what you've learned. She'll be really proud of you."

As he watched them dash into the house, Keith felt really good. He loved to play teacher. *I've got to do this sort of thing more often*, he thought. But he'd had such thoughts before.

As soon as he walked in the door, Joan blurted out, "*Now* you show up! You get to play outdoors while I slave over the hot stove. And then you show up late, as usual. So half the dinner is cold, and the other half is burnt. If I didn't have to feed the kids, I'd throw it all into the trash." She was shouting now, and she had obviously had a drink or two. The children slunk off to their rooms with scared, half-guilty looks. Keith felt the familiar knot returning to his stomach.

Long ago, when he had just finished his five obligatory years in the Navy nuclear program, Keith had felt like the king of the mountain. The whole world knew he had successfully completed the best engineering training program on the planet, and a small but promising company had snapped him up and given him what looked like a heaven-sent career. That was just eleven years ago, but it seemed like another lifetime. He had married Joan, who had promptly become pregnant. She'd had an interesting, well-paying career, but he'd persuaded her to leave it to take care of the kids. His salary could provide for them, and he'd proceeded to buy a Jaguar and a larger house than they'd really needed. But paying for them over time had made it seem workable.

For a while, things had gone well, although the difference between two incomes feeding two mouths and one income feeding three, then four had continually surprised Keith. Then one day, he had come home and announced that he had left his job. He'd had an argument with the boss, who had made what Keith considered a stupid technical decision. Keith's high technical standards would not allow him to stay on under such circumstances. "Don't worry," he had assured a worried Joan, "there are plenty of good jobs out there."

But Keith's precipitous action had resulted in a bad personnel record. His old company told potential employers that he was arrogant and a poor team player. For months, there were no job offers. Without medical insurance, they had to pay the full, exorbitant costs for the medical procedures to search endlessly for the source of Bud's mysterious illness. "Why are you always surprised by these problems?" Joan repeatedly yelled at Keith. "Why didn't you think about these things before you so casually walked out on a good job?" But she was afraid to push him too hard—he was so bipolar. Sometimes when he was late coming home at night, she feared she might get a call saying that he had thrown himself in front of a speeding subway train. Some days, that seemed like foolish nightmare; other times, she was not so sure.

Keith became increasingly frustrated, then downright scared. He knew that history majors and graduates of comparative literature often had trouble getting work, but not engineers. They always had several job options to choose from. He was completely unprepared to deal with his situation.

Finally, Keith saw a ray of light. Through his local engineering society chapter, he met and became close friends with Ralph Belasco. Belasco was fifteen years older than Keith, but they were kindred spirits, and Keith drew strength and hope from their monthly chapter meetings and the quick beers he had afterwards with a few members of the group. He was still a good engineer, and he was accepted as such.

Then a computer guru introduced him to Kim, who had a mundane job but a glorious dream. Kim's job took only eight or ten hours out of his day, which left him plenty of time to work on his dream: a Virtual Librarian! Keith, then Ralph, bought in on the dream, and one day Ralph had an idea. "Keith, the infotech company where I work has a lot of good people and is financially sound, but the top financial guy is very conservative. This has served the company well up to now, but they're beginning to worry that their competitors are getting fancy new equipment and that they may start falling behind. I think that's a legitimate worry, and I think that a Virtual Librarian may be just what they need. Why don't you and Kim come talk to Murph, our financial boss?"

Ralph set up a meeting, and Keith went in, suddenly filled with a new confidence. This was something he could do. But Murph McCarthy was no pushover. "Robertson, why should I take you on? I'm told you're hard to get along with and a poor team player. I already have some characters like that here. I don't need any more. If we undertake this development you're pushing, it would be an expensive long shot. You don't sound like the kind of person who could pull it off. Convince me I'm wrong."

Murph didn't know it, but he was playing right into Keith's strength; he had faced this approach before. "Mr. McCarthy, I survived and prospered under the toughest boss and the greatest technical challenge you can name. I satisfied Admiral Rickover and his people and was given good marks for overcoming unprecedented technical obstacles. There's no way you can outdo that challenge. With Kim's help, I can do this job."

Murph grinned inwardly but continued to snarl. "Okay, I'll give you both a chance. But you're coming in with two strikes against you. This is not the U.S. government, with unlimited funds and no accountability. We have limited money and limited time, which is really the same thing. You've got to live up to high standards and stay within your budget. Do it, and you're a hero. Fail, and you're just another unemployed bum."

Keith finally had a salary and medical insurance again, but the bills came in fast. He had no money in the bank, and he'd tapped out his mortgage and a big loan from Joan's father. ("And there's no more where that came from, young man!") Although the future looked promising, he could not even begin to climb out of the financial hole he had dug. Keith worried about Joan becoming an alcoholic, and she worried about him becoming suicidal. And the only thing that could save them was Kim's Virtual Librarian. Their future depended on making the software into a money-making reality.

MURPH

TUESDAY, APRIL 10: INFOPOWER'S MAIN CONFERENCE ROOM

InfoPower (IP) was one of a growing number of American companies that produced few tangible products. Its raw material and output was information. Its assets and tools were software programs and data files. It could take a subject like printing, and because of its knowledge of most of the world's printing facilities, it could show its clients how to improve print quality and save money at the same time. Sometimes this involved using a Singaporean printer for complex typography, a Swiss printer for glossy photo calendars, and a local print shop for quick turnaround on informal newsletters. But most of InfoPower's efforts focused on industrial and technological operations, like power plants and chemical processing facilities, that required not only information technology skills but also considerable scientific, engineering, and analytical prowess.

IP's closest competitors were Power to the People (P2P) and CyberTek (CTek), both of whom also dealt almost exclusively in information. IP liked to think of itself as the best, though the company constantly felt the others nipping at its heels. After IP employees had worked on a job for a while, the clients grew used to going to them for the latest drawings, material specifications, quality assurance programs, applicable code requirements, and the like. IP employees knew more about each client's plant than its owners did. They understood that the devil was in the details, and they were never too proud to dig for them, adding that salvation could be found there as well. Not only were picky, little details responsible for most unexpected problems, but it was also details that distinguished reliable operations from ones that repeatedly broke down.

Murph McCarthy was one of the two founders of InfoPower. He was the money man. Ralph Belasco was the techie and was generally seen as the visionary, the one who took the lead in defining the corporate mission. So a lot of the employees were surprised when they first heard that it was McCarthy who would give the troops a presentation on The Library, which was, after all, a primarily technical venture. But on second thought, most of them realized that few of the troops would question its technical aspects. They merely wanted assurances that this delightful toy was expected to add to, not endanger, the company's employee bonus kitty.

Murph was tough-minded, as a corporate CEO should be. He was a little guy, and the troops speculated that he'd probably had to fight to prove himself as a kid. He was far from handsome and always looked as if he had just discovered something outrageous. His eyes were abnormally wide, his brows arched high on his forehead, and his voice was high-pitched; it always seemed as if he were about to yell, "What the *hell* do you think you're doing?!" Just being in his presence got most people's hearts pounding. Murph was responsible for the fact that IP's offices, though fully adequate, were undistinguished and looked like hundreds of other offices in the city. But when you walked into a room where Murph was, there was never any question about who was the senior officer present.

Murph could scare hell out of an employee who had acted in a manner that he considered irresponsible, like the time he figured out that some of the programmers were working late most nights but charging only forty hours a week to the job. The programmers had argued, "We really got off track and were spinning our wheels for a while. It was our own stupidity. We can't charge the client for that." They had expected to be praised for their ethical stand.

Instead, Murph had roared, "Bullshit! I want every hour that every person works to be charged on the timesheet. If you think the company should swallow some of it, tell me, and I will decide. We've done that lots of times. But that's not the issue here. The issue is that you characters keep doing this over and over, job after job, and then when the next job comes in, we underbid it based on the phony history you've created."

"But if we charged all that time, we'd price ourselves off the market," the programmers countered.

Murph jumped on that one. "Aha! Now it comes out! The real issue. If we can't compete based on the actual hours we put in on the job, then we'd better figure out what to do about that. That's a more fundamental problem."

They all understood and agreed, but they never fully complied. It drove Murph nuts.

Murph worked all the time and expected the same from his employees and contractors. Keith knew other people like that, and they were generally nerds; they knew an incredible amount of information about some arcane corner of the computing and info management world, but they knew little else. Murph was different. He was widely read in history, literature, and the classics, though he was curiously disinterested in the arts. He didn't read for pleasure or as a diversion, and the idea of a hobby or an avocation was alien to him. He read because he wanted to apply as many of humanity's hard-won lessons as he could to the job that was his life. He often came across bits of information that he had his secretary copy and pass on to his team. Sometimes they were technical or managerial, but more often they were historical or even literary.

Murph's favorite gambit for squeezing the most out of a day was to work from 7:00 to 5:00, then catch a late-afternoon plane to the west coast. He'd schedule an evening meeting with a client, then catch the red-eye back home, arriving at the office a little after 7:00 AM. Outsiders wondered how he got such dedication from high-caliber people; why did they take it? The answer was surprisingly simple: he hired high-potential students right out of school and started offering them tasks of great responsibility and opportunity. Of course, the good ones leapt at the chance. Then, of course, the commitments were their own; they had said they could handle things, and they did. Murph didn't have to order them to work late nights and weekends. But if they didn't, they'd miss something, and meeting their commitments was tough enough without that.

Murph enjoyed taking on an exciting and risky venture as much as any of the engineers. This enjoyment showed itself today as he looked at the expectant faces before him and started his pitch at high intensity.

"As you know, this meeting is to tell you something about The Library, our latest major project. Those of you who have been speculating about what the "TL Project" is need speculate no more. There is an infinite number of questions you can ask about the design and operation of this amazing system, but that can best be done in one-on-one discussions after you've spent a few minutes experiencing the system for yourselves. The guys in Development have a job to do, so they can't spend all their time running a tourist attraction. But they've agreed to take on a certain number of you each day until everybody who wants to see it has seen it. I'll let them schedule that. Just sign up on the sheet on the bulletin board in front of the lab. They've agreed to put in a lot of evenings and weekends on this, so I urge you to take advantage of that. We've still got to log some chargeable time while all this is going on.

"Today, I want to talk about the question of why. Why are we taking on a project of this magnitude when a lot of our own money is at stake? I've been asked, doesn't this system just make file clerks out of high-priced people? That's an important question, and we've all got to understand the answer if the company is going to prosper in the years ahead."

Murph pulled a few three-by-five cards out of his shirt pocket, and his audience leaned forward, sensing that he was getting to the good stuff. Despite the company credo that information was digital and should be accessed electronically, Murph still used three-by-five cards. He was a fast learner. When he wanted to bone up on a subject, he got Ralph or someone else to bring him texts and papers about it, and the knowledge shortly became his. He owned it, he understood it, and he could work with it. And he had clearly done that this time.

"We say we sell engineering analysis and design. But engineers can no longer go out with a set of wrenches and a slide rule. More and more, we work with data and with highly sophisticated techniques for manipulating it. You all know that even on simple-sounding jobs with valves and pumps, we keep proving that taking a fundamental approach has proved to be the fastest way to get to a final answer. You calculate the system from first principles, starting with an infinitesimal volume and calculating the forces on it, the heat flowing into and out of it. You use an approach that sticks. One you don't have to keep redoing.

"That's what we're really selling: information and ways to handle it. And file folders are no longer adequate tools for controlling data. An outfit called Cuadra Associates compiled some statistics to describe the current situation. They wrote a report that says that one hundred billion documents are created each year in the U.S, and on the average, nineteen copies are made of *each one* and filed away somewhere. And that's data from 1994, so you know it's even worse now. The number of active files in a typical American company is growing by twenty-five percent each year—a hell of a lot faster than we are increasing our ability to deal with them. I'm told that the amount of knowledge available doubles every eighteen months. Anyone who understands how exponential functions works can appreciate what that means."

At this point, Murph fished around in his pocket and pulled out another index card, more battered and dog-eared than the others. "Let me read you something. This was written by a gent named Denis Diderot in 1755. That's about 250 years ago, for those of you brought up on new math. This is what he wrote: 'The number of books will grow continually, and one can predict that a time will come when it will be almost as difficult to learn anything from books as from direct study of the whole universe. It will be almost as convenient to search for some bit of truth concealed in nature as it will be to find it hidden away in an immense multitude of bound volumes.'"

He put the cards back in his pocket. He was ready to quote from memory, to show that he knew the statistics and took them seriously. "You want some scary numbers? A typical large company loses a document every twelve seconds. Three percent of all documents are incorrectly filed, and one out of every fourteen documents filed is lost forever. Moreover, in most cases, there is no system for trashing documents once they are no longer needed, so they keep piling up and burying the urgent ones. And once you get involved in a lawsuit—and aren't we always?—if you can't find the documents you need, or if documents you should have trashed show up to embarrass you ... well, you get the idea.

"And do you realize how much it costs to have information on paper—mountains of it—instead of on a little DVD? Did you know that the documentation for a 747 airliner weighs more than the airplane? Some of our clients spent fifty to a hundred thousand dollars per year just shipping printed updates of their documentation to various customers. That's just the postage money!

"Now, think of all the information in your head that you can call up when you need it. Where would you be if you suddenly found you couldn't remember where the bathrooms were or how to integrate a differential equation? Well, a corporation needs a Corporate Memory for the same reasons that you need your personal memory bank. If a company's memory resides only in the heads and the desk drawers of its employees, it's not only degraded when people leave, but it might as well not exist at all unless each employee is fully aware of what's in everyone else's files."

Murph was coming to the punch line. "Any outfit as dependent as we are on information decides at some point that they'd better pull it together and make all their data retrievable. And as you know, we did that a couple of years ago."

His voice had been smooth and soothing up until that point, so everyone jumped when he suddenly roared, "*Or maybe you didn't notice!* Because very little happened when that order went out. Sure, the tech library did a good job of getting the stuff on their shelves entered into the new digital system. But you guys didn't come in with much new stuff. All the information was still squirreled away in your desks or stashed in some folder in the back of a file drawer."

Murph was now shouting at top volume. "*Such information might as well not even exist! It's not part of the Corporate Memory! We're getting corporate Alzheimer's! And it's going to kill us if we don't do something about it!*"

The room was dead silent except for the quiet shuffling of people squirming in their seats—people who knew that Murph was right and felt guilty as they recalled the papers in their own files that nobody else knew anything about. After an uncomfortably long pause, Murph resumed his oration, assuming a firm but more avuncular tone.

"I don't expect to solve this problem by calling you all sinners. There are other people who make a living doing that. I'm convinced that the solution lies in persuading each of you that adding to the Corporate Memory is vital to doing your own job—I repeat, *your own job*. So that you'll blast one of your colleagues when you discover, too late, that he had some information that could have saved your tail.

"I am adding a subroutine to our word-processing software; after you type each letter, memo, or report, it will ask, *Do you want to enter this into Corporate Memory?* If it's unfinished or otherwise inappropriate, you click 'no,' and that's it. If you choose 'yes,' it will ask you to suggest keywords or other search identifiers. Who knows better than you what the key points in your documents are? We should have done this long ago. And I'm having our librarian look into getting more powerful, more flexible search software. If you pick up other documents on trips or copy them out of journals, you can scan them electronically and enter them into the system. Don't bother to clean up after the character-reading software; the documents will be ninety to ninety-five percent okay, and that's good enough for retrieval."

And then Murph paused. His long silences always effectively refocused everyone's attention. All his employees were really listening now.

"But the big step we are taking now is to create a virtual reality library, which we call The Library, or TL for short. This will make information retrieval fun, but that's just a side benefit. Incidentally, I don't want to find any of you characters treating The Library like an arcade game. It's not a toy. Virtual reality is so convincing that a shrink in California named Ralph Lamson has found that he can cure cases of acrophobia just by having people walk out a door onto a virtual plank suspended high in the air over water. These people know on one level that they're not in any real danger, but it's real enough to cure them.

"I've been asked to warn you that virtual reality can be a very powerful experience—sometimes it's seriously disorienting. Researchers in this field have found cases in which people have had flashbacks and moments of panic long after their exposure to VR. It's apparently something like the after-effects of overusing hallucinogenic drugs, although I'm not in a position to talk about that from personal experience.

"The point is, I'm trying to make it clear that this is serious stuff. There is no place in this company for file clerks. Handling information is our profession. No one is too smart or too well educated to do that. It's our life-blood, our bread and butter. We're putting a lot of effort—and a lot of expensive technology—into making locating and retrieving information as effective, simple, and natural as we can. And our model for how best to do this is the way in which you find information in your own brains. That's going to be our guideline: how do we do it in our own heads?

"We're looking at all kinds of ways to make the abstract process of pawing through file folders more visual, more natural. It should be like wandering through a garden—or, better yet, through a museum where each hall branches into different subjects related to the one you just left. All of this is very exploratory, and TL will continue to be a work-in-progress. So don't be upset by the changes you see from time to time. Just give us feedback on whether the changes make it easier or harder to find what you need.

"One more thing, and I'm going to say it twice so that you'll really get it. There's an old Sufi saying, 'What I tell you three times is true.' Well, I'm not going to say it three times; you characters are supposed to be smart enough to get it on the second pass. Here it is: TL is not worth the money it will cost us." He paused. "I'll put it another way: *the product, the library I've been describing, cannot justify the money and effort we will have to put into it.*" He paused again. "Got that?"

"So why are we doing this? I want you all to understand the answer. TL is just the first step in a long journey we have to take. You remember when not so long ago, we decided we were going to have to get rid of our typewriters and put everybody, including the secretaries, on computers? Remember? We all felt pretty uncomfortable with that for a while. But now it's hard to believe that we ever thought of doing it another way.

"Well, this is another such historic occasion. This is the direction we have to go to survive. We can only see the first step 'through a glass darkly,' as the Bible says. So we'll feel uncomfortable at first as we try to learn how to use The Library. What I'm trying to tell you is that we dare not get too comfortable with it. We're going to have to move forward again toward even more sophisticated and arcane techniques and procedures. And so everything we are doing now is with that in mind. The long view. Only if we think that way can we justify the money and effort we are going to put into this new system.

"I am thoroughly convinced that this company will either become more and more proficient at finding and using information or become non-competitive and irrelevant. I'm doing what I can; it's up to you characters to make it work. Now I'm going to turn the mic over to our chief technical officer, Ralph Belasco, who will give you a glimpse of some of the things we may have to think about while we're trying to get comfortable with The Library. There's some pretty wild stuff here, and most of it will never come to pass. But we're going to have to learn to think about and deal with things like these."

Ralph Belasco was not a spellbinder like Murph. He was sixty—an old man in this business. He was not fat, but he put little effort into keeping fit, so he was a bit pudgy. The cut of his gray hair and his clothing were casual; it was obvious that he gave little thought to style. Keith always pictured him emphasizing points by poking a short forefinger into a circuit diagram, a system sketch, or the chest of a listener. His colleagues claimed that if Ralph ever lost that finger, he could apply for Workman's Comp. He was not a natural orator, and he generally picked the simplest and most common words or phrases rather than choosing something more colorful and evocative. But he was highly regarded as a technician by all who knew him, and his reputation for being straightforward and honest as well earned him a respectful and attentive audience. He picked up a large pile of technical papers, magazines, and technical books and came up to the microphone.

"I don't have any fancy PowerPoint presentation," he began. "Murph told me this morning that it might be useful for me to tell you about some of the similar ideas and techniques that are already showing up on the Web and in the technical journals. None of these have been proven yet, and many of them are downright kooky. But these are the kinds of things we'll either be trying out or rejecting in the next five to ten years, so you'd better start thinking about them now. I'll just toss some of them out there in no particular order. Tomorrow there'll be more; a week later, there'll be even more. So the ones I'm about to describe are not necessarily ones you'll ever see again. They're just the ones on my screen right now." *All right already*, thought Keith. *Just tell us*. He could never get used to Ralph's defensive, qualified intros.

"You all remember how reluctant we were to get everybody wired up into an office network. Around the time we got used to that and started wondering how we'd ever operated all isolated, we discovered that we should have used optical fiber connections rather than wires. That's the way it's going to be from now on, except the changes will be faster. But I guess Murph covered that. So let me just mention some specifics." *At last!* thought Keith. He never asked himself why he spent so much psychic energy sweating over everyone else's actions. It took almost as much effort for him to listen to a talk as it did to give one. He always wanted speakers to do things a little differently. And faster.

"My earliest experience with office computers was when I first went to work in the early 1960s," said Ralph. "That was before some of you were born, but it was not so long ago in terms of industrial development. We had pads of paper specially designed for scrawling rows of zeros and ones. Those were the only permissible symbols—zeroes and ones. We were programming in machine language. Then we took those papers down to a computer service company a few blocks away, and an operator used a machine to punch square holes through long, skinny cards that we called IBM cards. Then we fed these cards to a computer that printed out miles of green-striped paper with data on it. This paper was usually delivered to us the next morning in what they called 'batch mode.' There was no such thing as interacting with a computer on a real-time basis. In fact, our first setup sent the IBM cards to Philadelphia for processing. It was a big step forward when we were able to get it done locally.

"We couldn't see how this technology could ever be any better than the slide rules we depended on. Hard as it may be for some of you to imagine working under such conditions, it's harder yet to imagine what it will be like as many years in the future. But we have to imagine the future before we can produce it. So I'll just tease you with some things that people are already talking about. It's too late to come up with these ideas—they're already here. Start imagining what might come next."

He picked up a newspaper clipping. "Here's one: 'PhotoBubbles,' the Web's first 360-degree photographs, allow the casual user to look at spherical snapshots, or "immersive representations," of everything from England's Westminster Abbey to opening night at Atlanta's Centennial Village.' This idea is already commercially available. And here's another: kids who object to dissecting frogs and cats in biology class for religious or other reasons can now do it with an interactive, virtual reality CD-ROM. No live animals present.

"Here's an article headlined, 'The hottest new item in entertainment is Virtual Reality Fishin'—a chance to net a trophy fish while on dry land.' And it shows a guy sitting in one of those big chairs they have on deep-sea fishing boats, holding a fishing pole and looking at a TV. The article explains, 'Any rod can be attached to the "game line"—which runs inside a large box, and scores each opponent— and the pull on the rod is matched to a large TV screen that shows an actual fishing scene.' The sailfish jumps out of the water. It runs away. It comes back. Just like in "real life." What often starts out as a lark quickly becomes deadly serious. Now, this idea is already on the market. It's on the boardwalk at Ocean City. I've never tried it myself, but I have played a few rounds of virtual golf, which is the same sort of thing.

"Here's one from *Scientific American*, October, 1996. Ancient history. 'Controlling Computers with Neural Signals: Electrical impulses from nerves and muscles can command computers directly.' And here's a two-volume special issue on mediated reality from the *International Journal of Human-Computer Interaction* that talks about 'personal, wearable imaging devices with intelligence that arises from the existence of a human user in the feedback loop of a computational process.'

"Here's an MSNBC news item from October 7, 1999: 'Artificial and Real Nerve Cells Linked. Using $7.50-worth of electrical parts, scientists hook up an artificial neuron to biological nerve cells extracted from a lobster.' The resulting neuron network transmitted signals back and forth just like the real thing—one small step toward a bionic future. And from BBC News Online the next day: 'Computer Uses Cat's Brain to See. U.S. scientists have wired a computer to a cat's brain and created videos of what the animal saw.' And a Wired News Report, September 30, 1999: 'Researchers have bioengineered three-dimensional, beating heart tissue inside a simulated space environment. The tissue was created from neonatal rat cells using a device called the bioreactor.'

"And so on. You can see that I've only skimmed this stack of papers. And this stack is just a random sample of a few days' news. But don't start getting excited over this stuff—this is history. Engineers like you got excited about these ideas five or ten years ago. What are you going to make five or ten years from now? You should be working on it now. Dan Johnson of *The Futurist* says, 'You can't predict the future, but you can change its course.' That's our job here. Ray Kurzweil, who knows as much about these things as anyone, predicts that by 2019—and that's just around the corner—a one thousand dollar computing device (in 1999 dollars) will have approximately the computational ability of the human brain. And ten years after that, the same dollars will buy a gadget one thousand times more powerful. If machines are that much smarter than people, what will our relationship with them be like? Some wise guy said, 'If we're lucky, they'll let us hang around as pets.' Well, personally, I'd like to keep ahead of that situation.

"So the punch line is that TL, wonderful as it is, is already out of date and growing more obsolete every hour. It's our job to not only keep up with this situation but to ride its bow-wave. So fasten your seatbelts and prepare for an exciting ride."

And he turned and walked briskly out of the room, not wanting anything to spoil his unexpected eloquence. The others got up and left quietly, exchanging only a few words in low tones.

Keith just sat there for a while. He felt strangely excited, but he was suddenly very tired. This wasn't going to be easy.

TUESDAY, APRIL 10, EVENING: THE ROBERTSONS'S HOME

Nobody had picked up on Murph's "TL" moniker. It was too cold and stuffy, too front-officey. But everyone was intrigued by The Librarian, who was dubbed Lib or Libby. So that became the name for the whole project.

Keith was beginning to feel better about Lib. He could see that working with her will be different from working with regular search engines like Google. Lib asked more innovative and insightful questions, and she sometimes left Keith feeling as if he'd just been on a date with a woman who knew more about his work than he did. It brought back some of the uncomfortable feelings from his dating days, which he'd almost forgotten since he'd married Joan.

In fact, he'd had a nightmare in which Lib and Joan and some vague, Frankensteinian monster were all mixed up, and he awoke in a cold sweat. It was long and detailed, and it didn't make any sense. Keith couldn't remember any of the details well enough to describe them. He tried to write the dream down to encourage his memory, but all he could remember clearly was the intense feeling of dread and foreboding. He couldn't shake it. Crazy as it was, it had a powerful feeling of reality and urgency about it. Keith gave up trying to figure out what it meant and just tried to get over it. His colleagues were mostly happily optimistic about Lib, and Keith tried to dismiss his funny foreboding as a reflection of his own problems with women.

He casually asked Kim about it, as he would have felt funny talking about it with Joan. As he often did, Kim asked a critical question in return: "Would you feel any different if Lib were a man?"

"And acted the same way?" replied Keith.

"Yeah. All the same words, same reactions, but from a man."

"Gee, I don't know," said Keith. "Good question. But I really don't know. Don't you ever feel a little apprehensive about Lib, Kim? Is she just another piece of software to you?"

"Instead of a piece of tail, you mean?" grinned Kim.

"No, no," said Keith. "That's really not my problem. I'm sure about that now. I guess I would feel the same apprehension if she were a man. Some of her questions and her suggestions are uncanny. Don't you have a problem with that, Kim?"

"Yeah, I do. I know what you're talking about. But of course, that's what we're trying for—something way beyond today's search engines. Anyway, there's nothing I can do about it, so I go on with my work."

Keith had been ruminating on these thoughts since he got home. Joan, apparently recognizing his mood, held her tongue, and they ate dinner in near silence. This was not an unusual occurrence in their marriage, and both of them took it as a good sign that their relationship did not require them to make conversation when they would rather be curled up inside their own heads.

Keith's thoughts wandered into more personal territory. A few gray hairs had recently started to appear, and they had not escaped Joan's notice. *Damn*, he thought, *I'm going to look just like Dad.* He had been determined not to let that happen, yet here it was. And he was still in his mid-forties. *Well, I may not be able to prevent inherited baldness*, he thought grimly. *But by God, I don't have to develop that potbelly of his. Exercise, that's all it takes. I can't start right now, of course, but after we get this new library working...*

He knocked off the mental flagellation and tried to tell Joan about Lib and all the incredible futures they were exploring. But his words felt so mundane that they couldn't possibly convey what he felt. So he stopped mid-sentence, frustrated. She looked into his face. It was positively radiant. "I'm sure it's amazing, hotshot. I'm really glad you're doing it." And she leaned over and kissed him on the cheek. "But now I've got to go get some shuteye. I've had a busy day." And she headed off upstairs, sighing to herself as she realized that Keith would never ask her to tell him about her busy days. *Husbands never do*, she thought. *I guess that's just the way it is. The bastards!*

Keith marveled at the way Joan had apparently concluded that their financial problems were about to dissipate, and he felt some of the old marital warmth beginning to return. She seemed less bitter, the vicious attacks were less frequent and less intense, and he thought she was drinking less. But he couldn't really be sure about any of that since he wasn't home much.

Of course he was happy about these changes, but perversely, they also seemed to intensify his anxiety; Lib was still very much a work in progress. Curiously, he aimed his plaintive wishes and prayers at Lib rather than Kim. He knew that Kim would do his best and that his best would be very good. He had confidence in Kim. But he worried irrationally that Lib would let him down—somehow, any failures would be *her* fault, not Kim's. Murph and IP had given Keith a second chance, and he was tremendously grateful for that. He knew that a lot of people never got second chances. But all of that just increased the pressure on *him*. The higher they all flew, the harder they'd fall. And the possibility of ever getting a third chance was slim.

. The characters in Human Resources tried to get him to talk with Dr. Gillespie, the company shrink. But there was no way he would do that. Being personally confused was one thing; officially going on the record as a psycho was something else. He didn't need that. He was surprised to see Ginger McGee walk out of Gillespie's office one day; he'd always known she was a little bubbly, but did this mean she was really coming unwrapped? He was determined that no one should ever see *him* coming out of that door!

He thought about the early astronauts, sitting in a highly unreliable rocket with a history of explosions, misfires, and failures. The whole world had watched on TV, praying, *Dear God, don't let them be killed.* But Keith had read that the astronauts themselves had prayed, *Dear God, don't let me screw up.* And he could understand that. He surely could.

FRIDAY, APRIL 13: THE ROBERTSONS'S HOME

Keith was only mildly annoyed with Joan. "Aw, honey, don't make a big deal out of it. I just asked the Rubins over for a drink before we go out to eat tonight. We don't have to do anything fancy."

Joan didn't let him off too easily. "You can say that, but I don't see you running the vacuum."

Though she said it lightly and without bitterness, such comments always touched off a sense of guilt in Keith. *I've left her practically the whole job of keeping the house and raising our kids*, he mused, *and the time I spend with them is all the fun time—picnics, visits to the wonderful Washington museums, occasional weekend trips. She has to do all the hard stuff—talks with teachers, visits to the emergency room.* He had learned several lessons during his five years with Admiral Rickover, the crusty king of the nuclear navy. Rickover had taught him that having a vocation—as opposed to a mere job—was something of a miracle. It was like being in love, he'd said. And wives seldom appreciate a rival love. But marriage had taught Keith that there were times when you should hold your tongue and not bite back. He knew this was one of those times.

Since neither of them had their hearts in it, the argument was already dying out by the time the doorbell rang. Joan let in their friends Bob and Maggie Rubin. They were in their late forties, a few years older than Keith and Joan. Bob was a computer engineer for a small company in town. He was widely read and could talk philosophy, religion, or metaphysics with the best of them. He and Keith could keep that up all night, and they both enjoyed it immensely. Maggie was a tall woman with a down-to-earth manner but an uncommon dignity. She made little attempt to look cute or glamorous, but her strong, handsome face and bearing always commanded respect. She followed and understood all the conversational interplay, and she had some interesting ideas of her own, which she would voice if asked. But she was usually content to let "the boys" run with the conversational ball, slipping in an occasional wry comment to Joan under her breath. This style of interaction suited all four of them, and they got together often. They subscribed to the local theater together, which was quite good, and they often preceded performances with meals at the many ethnic restaurants nearby.

It didn't take long to see why Keith had initiated this get-together although there was no play scheduled. He was bubbling over with stories about Libby, and he totally monopolized the conversation until he got a high sign from Joan.

"Why don't we all go out on the deck," she asked. "That's where I'd intended to set up some snacks. But Keith here took off with his sales pitch before anyone could sit down, and I haven't even gotten drink orders yet."

The Robertsons's one-story, two-bedroom, red brick house in Bethesda, Maryland looked like a typical commuter's home in that upper-middle-class suburb of Washington DC. Although there were only two basic house designs in their eighty-five-house development, they came in right- and left-hand models. Some of the brickwork was painted and some was not, and some houses had a bit of clapboard in place of the brick. Through the years, the varied landscaping had grown up; some owners had made bedrooms out of the attached garages, added porches, or even added second floors. The original "development" look had been pretty well overcome. Keith's eighty-foot-wide lot sloped down toward the back fence, so the simple, unpainted, wooden deck that he had added onto the back of the house was about seven feet in the air. It looked out onto the hundred-yard-wide strip of tall trees that shielded the fifth hole of the Columbia Country Club's golf course. The open deck was shady and pleasant in the hot, Washington summers, and the Robinsons used it a lot. After the food, drinks, and seating arrangements had been resolved, Joan spoke up. "Keith got his licks in," she began, "and now I've got something I'd like to get your opinions on." She was clutching a paperback book.

Keith looked a bit surprised, and Bob simply said, "Go ahead, Joan."

"It's this book I picked up the other day. It's called *Psychic Discoveries Behind the Iron Curtain*." She handed it to Bob. "I'd really like for you to take a look at it and return it whenever you're finished."

"Oh, *that*," sighed Keith

"It's pretty wild," continued Joan. "It's about ESP—mind-reading—and PK, which stands for psychokinesis—making physical things move or change with mental power alone. They call all that stuff 'psi,' you know, for the first letter of the Greek word 'psyche.'" Joan had taken on her best schoolteacher voice.

Keith cut in before Bob could reply. "Aw, that's a lot of crap—witchcraft, black magic. You see a lot of that kind of folklore in countries that aren't fully modernized. When you actually check into those things, they always turns out to be nothing but old wives' tales."

"What about it, Joan?" asked Bob. "Is that what the book says?"

"No, it really doesn't. The authors are college graduates and respected writers. They spent five years in Russia and other Iron Curtain countries during the late sixties, and they sent reports back from a big, international parapsychology conference in Moscow. It was around 1968, as I remember. They interviewed a lot of scientists who were exploring this stuff, and they talk about that in the book. There are some interesting pictures in here, too. I found the whole thing fascinating."

"Did they ever explain how people move things with their minds?" asked Bob.

"I don't think anyone knows. But in this book, a woman moves matchboxes, pill bottles, a compass needle, and other stuff without ever touching them."

"Aw, that's an old magician's trick," objected Keith. "They do it with fine threads. Or they blow softly through nearly closed lips. I saw a magician do that at a birthday party when I was a kid. Everybody was wowed, but I could see he was blowing the stuff around."

"No, this is different," countered Joan. "This book is loaded with references, including legitimate, European, scientific journals. The other day, I called Chris Bird about this stuff, and he said that when he was a *Time-Life* correspondent in Belgrade, he interviewed and corresponded with a lot of the people in the book. They swear their reports are accurate. They've had some pretty hotshot scientists in on those PK tests. One of them—a respected brain researcher who has published widely abroad—developed a very sensitive electromagnetic instrument that could detect someone's bioenergy, as they call it, from twelve feet away. He rigged up this woman Kulagina with electrodes, like they do with astronauts, and found that she generated fifty times more electrical energy at the back of her brain than she did at the front, which is very unusual. When she started to rev up her mind to move the objects on the table, there was a huge amount of energy in the region of the brain associated with sight. Sometimes she became temporarily blind after the tests. And her heartbeat increased to 240 beats per minute, which is four times a normal heart rate!

"And when the stuff started to move, the brain experts saw something they had never seen before. Her heart and her brain waves began to pulse together, and the magnetic field outside of her body also pulsed at the same frequency. And then it became focused in the direction of her gaze. The magnetic field created by her body was almost as strong as the magnetic field of the earth!" Joan was now sitting on the edge of her chair, her face flushed with excitement.

"After the tests, she was exhausted. She had almost no pulse for a while, and she lost four pounds in half an hour. Her heartbeat was erratic, her blood sugar was high, and her pancreas and spleen and all those other little giblets were disturbed. That doesn't come from pulling on threads."

Everyone was quiet for a moment. Then Joan asked, "What do you make of this, Bob?" She knew that he was usually intrigued by anything he didn't understand. He collected his thoughts, then said, "Well, Joan, it does seem to tie in with some other things that Maggie and I have heard lately. You remember that I talked about the Silva Mind Control course last time we were together? I met a couple who had taken the course, and they said it was an experience they'd never forget." He paused. "Maggie and I signed up to take it next week. Right here in Bethesda."

"Do they give you the power to cloud men's minds, like The Shadow?" cracked Keith.

"No, it's not about controlling other people's minds; it's not *Manchurian Candidate* stuff. It's about learning to control your own mind. I don't know much about it yet, but it sounds impressive."

"Is it any different from Edgar Cayce, or est, or any of those other kooky seminars and workshops you've gone to?" asked Keith.

"I guess we'll see," said Maggie with a smile. It was the first and only thing she said that evening.

"Well, *I* want to hear all about it when you're finished," said Joan emphatically, and Keith felt that her comment was aimed at him more than at Bob. He didn't say anything. He had a lot of respect for Bob, but he just couldn't see any basis for believing that people could push things around in the physical world just by thinking about them.

KIM

WEDNESDAY, APRIL 18: IP DEVELOPMENT LAB

Keith figured that enough time had passed that he would have no trouble getting time to use Libby for an extended trial run. But when he got to the lab, there was even more activity than there had been before. All of the regular tech gang were there, plus a couple of new people Keith had never seen before. There was a lot of joking and laughing, but nobody was loafing—everybody seemed to have a task and was busy doing it. Kim was clucking over them all like a mother hen and was even jollier than usual. He greeted Keith effusively.

Keith was baffled. "I thought you characters were supposed to have this all wrapped up days ago. What's going on?"

Kim was delighted to respond. "We did wrap it up days ago—better than spec, sooner than scheduled, unfortunately somewhat over cost. But nobody's mad; everybody's tickled pink. So now we are transcending good, surpassing excellent, and heading where no man has ever gone before. Sorry—where no *one* has ever gone before." He cast a jaundiced eye Ginger's way.

"Cut the bull and tell me what's going on. In simple terms an Earthling can understand."

Kim came back down to earth. He was still happy, but now he was also dead serious. "We are really making an important next step," he intoned solemnly. "No shit, this is really great. We are modifying the software so that the system will learn from every usage. It will learn which search strategies are most effective and what each user means when they say various terms. Like a smart person, it will get to know its users individually. And it'll just keep getting better and better!" His face positively glowed.

Keith was only mildly impressed. "I've already got that on my desktop Mac—commercial software that learns. DiskExpress sorts files into active, sporadic, and dormant categories based on my personal use patterns. Then it arranges the files on the disk so that the most active files are most accessible—it minimizes access times. Is that the kind of thing you're talking about?"

"That's only the first step. The key thing is that the software will evolve, like a species. Specie? Whatever. It will evolve. We'll start with a one-celled critter and end up with Albert Einstein ... and beyond."

"Well, before we get to 'beyond,' let me ask a simple, country-boy question. At the very beginning, Lib was surprisingly fluent. Her sentences were smooth, colloquial ... you know, like any gal you might meet. Now I hear that she sometimes struggles with language and seems at a loss for words. Is that your idea of progress?"

"You bet! Let me explain. For expediency, we started out by just feeding recorded speeches into the system. The software decided which of those speeches she should feed back. So the speeches could be as breezy and casual as you like, since they were pre-recorded by programmers. A good example is something like, 'Um, that's a toughie. Do you mean X, or is it more like Y? Which do you mean?' That forces the user to select between two options she's chosen. Or rather, that *we've* chosen. See what I mean? That's the sorta thing you get when you phone in for train or airplane schedules. We intend to do better than that."

"Yeah, but in Lib's case, why did it get worse?"

"We decided that having Lib just choose from a few canned answers would not allow much flexibility for growth. So we scrapped the pre-recorded tapes and substituted Kurzweil's synthetic speech. Ray Kurzweil introduced that to computers in the late 1950s—it was later quite popular on the old Apple III, for instance. We felt that as we got smarter, this would give us more elbow room to let Lib grow. We're just beginning to learn how to do that. It's an important step, and Lib'll be somewhat inarticulate for a while—like a pre-teen without much vocabulary trying to get beyond 'like' and 'y'know.'"

"Okay, but you said she will evolve. How do you make her do that? And what do you really mean by evolve? How is evolving any different from just learning? I'm not sure I can picture Libby turning into One Beer Al."

Kim took a deep breath. "Do you know anything about Tom Ray and his evolving computer viruses? Or John Holland? Have you read Kevin Kelly's *Out of Control* or Steve Levy's *Artificial Life*? Have you heard about any of the evolution studies that guys are doing with little computer programs—GAs, Holland calls them, for genetic algorithms?"

"Whoa, hold on. I'm just a simple mechanical engineer, remember? I've heard some of the words and some of the names you mentioned, but that's about as far as I go. I sure can't say I understand any of it. Is it possible for somebody with my background—or lack of background—to understand this stuff?"

"Okay," said Kim. "You wanna get serious? I'll talk 'til you're numb, and then you can go away and come back later. There's a lot of background for this stuff; I'll just start by giving you a little of it. Let's start with evolution. What's evolution? Ask Joe Sixpack, he'll tell you: survival of the fittest. What does it mean to be fit? It comes down to having the ability to survive. That doesn't tell you much. It sort of implies that the tough guys kill all the weaklings and they have tough kids, and so the race gets tougher. That kinda makes capitalism a law of nature, eh? Well, there's a lot more to it than that.

"For instance, there's a geneticist from Harvard by the name of John Cairns who claims that the environment sometimes causes mutations in E. coli bacteria that influence all future generations. That's what Lamarck called inheritance of acquired characteristics, and that has always been a no-no with Darwinians. Well, another biologist named Barry Hall then published experiments in which he challenged the bacteria with antibiotics or something, and they mutated at a rate one hundred million times faster than what Mr. Darwin might have calculated based on random, chance mutations. Furthermore, these mutations weren't random. The bacteria weren't just mutating in all kinds of ways, hoping to stumble on a survivable, useful mutation. The researchers sequenced the E. coli DNA—and don't ask me how they do that, I'm no biologist—and they found that the only mutations that had occurred were those that were needed. The other parts of the DNA were unchanged. Somehow, the bacteria figured out how to change themselves in just the right way to survive. That's real evolution."

"But how does all that tie in with what we're doing here?" asked Keith.

"I'm trying to show you that evolution is much more than just learning," said Kim. "Lib doesn't have offspring, but she can evolve like the Model T Ford evolved into the Lincoln Continental. You know what makes a supercomputer super? Those great big suckers they use to study weather and atomic bombs? They have hundreds of little computers all working in parallel. One of the tricks we used with Lib was to put lots of different kinds of search procedures to work on the same problem. That's an old librarian's trick, but the difference here is that Lib compares the results each time and studies which parts of which search procedures were most effective. You with me so far?"

"Yeah, but I'm not sure where you're taking me," said Keith.

"Let me go back to a guy named Tom Ray and another named John Holland. They played around with little tiny computer programs that they allowed to evolve. The goal was to perform a simple 'sort' routine—you know, like arranging a group of words in alphabetical order—and the original program to do this had eighty lines of instructions. Any program that did the task with less than eighty lines was rewarded by being reproduced, and programs that didn't were killed off prematurely. And these little programming routines actually invented program sex, in a way. They combined and kept the best parts of each program. It's like how the DNA in each of our parents combines to make us. Eventually, they got down to a twenty-two-line program that sorted more effectively than any program written by humans. How about that?!"

"That's pretty cool, all right," admitted Keith.

"One of the things that baffled the logicians is that if event A caused event B, and B caused event C, and then through feedback, event C caused event A, then event A was both a cause and an effect of what was happening. And that was true of all the other inputs as well. This drove some of the theoretickers wiggy. It's particularly frustrating if you want to control the whole process."

"I can see how it would be," mused Keith, who identified.

Kim forged on. "Now, if you've got all these causes going in and all these effects changing the causes, it literally becomes impossible to calculate how to control things. The solution came from two unrelated fields about twenty years apart. There was a steelworking plant, where ingots of hot steel were rolled into huge sheets. At least six factors controlled how thick the sheets were, and all of these factors changed significantly during the time a single sheet was being rolled, so the sheets always came out too thick in some places and too thin in others. Steelworkers spent decades trying to control the variables. But when they raised the temperature of the ingot, for instance, the traction of the rollers on the sheet changed. Each variable changed the others. Then some gent figured out that if they just controlled *one* of the variables, the others would necessarily follow. And it worked out just fine."

"That's pretty surprising," said Keith.

"Yeah, but it seems to be a general law."

"How do you know that?"

"About twenty years earlier, a guy named Hayek in the Austrian School of Economics found that people had been trying to control various components of the economy, and they had been failing miserably. So Hayek said, let's just control one variable, *price*, and the variables related to it will follow. Even the variables we don't know about will follow. It worked. So this principle seems to exist all over, and it is part of what we put into Lib."

Keith had to think about that. "I guess you've given me about all I can absorb for a while, Kim. Thanks for the 'Libby for Dummies' seminar."

"Any time, Keith. The only really important point is that Lib will learn in the old-fashioned way, and she will adapt her behavior to use what she learns. And then, from time to time, she will evolve drastically different ways of doing her work. They'll be ways we can't predict. And she won't have the same personality anymore. Later, if we try to back-engineer the design of her systems, we'll be amazed and confused and surprised by what we find. The system will no longer look like what we designed. She'll be a whole new creation, like the child that suddenly becomes an adult. And not the adult you expected or planned, but something new, frustrating, and yet glorious."

"I can hardly wait, Kim. Looking forward to it."

"Don't get too firm a picture in your mind, Keith; I can guarantee there will be surprises."

He couldn't have been more prophetic

FRIDAY, APRIL 20: KIM'S OFFICE

Many a stricken lass sighed over Kim Lee from afar; they all considered him the answer to their prayers. He was handsome, funny, cool, and obviously smart, but not nerdy. The only problem was that he was seldom seen outside the confines of his office. He almost never even went to the building cafeteria, preferring to throw an order toward anyone else headed that way: "Bring me a sub and a black coffee, willya please?" He was usually already at work when people got to the office, and he was still at work when they left.

This lifestyle left Kim almost no time for dating. Yet no one believed he was gay. Like many others—though more than most—he was just dedicated to his job. And no one knew any more than that about him. No one had visited his home or knew anything about his family. It was commonly understood that he was a very private person.

So Keith was jolted when he walked by Kim's office late one night and heard heartfelt sobs. He couldn't imagine Kim crying. The door was open, and Kim heard Keith's footsteps and looked up.

They were both embarrassed. Finally, Keith blurted out, "What happened? What's the matter?"

"It's my dad," sobbed Kim. "He's dying."

There was nothing for Keith to say, and he was wise enough to realize it. He just stood there. "I guess I always thought he'd just go on living forever," said Kim, more to himself than to Keith.

"Yeah, I know," said Keith. "I was the same way when my old man died a couple of years ago. You hear about other people's parents dying, and you think you understand. You think you know how they feel. But then, when it happens to you and people tell you they're sorry, you want to shout, 'No! You don't really know. This is different. He's my father. He wasn't like everybody else. He was …'" His voice broke. Tears were welling up in his eyes. He still had not fully recovered.

After a moment, Keith said, "Tell me about him, Kim. He must be quite a guy to have raised someone like you. He must be very proud of you."

"*No*," Kim shouted, almost angrily. "It's not like that at all. It's like you said before. He's not like anyone else. You can't understand this."

Keith was confused and a little hurt. He was learning not to talk when he didn't know what to say, so there was a long silence. Then he said, "You're my very best friend, Kim. You've got to talk with somebody. Not now, if you're not ready. But before long, you may want to. I'd like to understand. I'll try."

They both had tears in their eyes now, which was equally unusual for both of them. After a long silence, Keith turned to walk away. But Kim rose, put his hand on Keith's shoulder, and said softly, "You're right, Keith. I gotta do it. Will you listen? Sit down. I'll try to tell you.

"My father is a tenth- or twelfth-generation potter in Korea. He was designated by the government as a National Treasure. I know that doesn't mean anything in America, but believe me, in Korea it's a big deal. You know, the Smithsonian Museum recently had this big exhibit on Japanese pottery. There was a lot of shit in the papers about how great the Japanese potters are and how much pottery means to their culture. Well, let me tell you something. Japan had no good potters until the seventeenth century. Beginning in about 1640, a conquering Japanese warlord kidnapped the best Korean potters and brought them to Japan. Most of the famous Japanese potters today are descended from those old, Korean masters. My dad is one of them. Except that his father left Japan and returned to Korea. Most of them didn't.

"It's incredible! Four thousand years ago, Korean potters were turning out beautiful works of art, firing glazes of all kinds and colors in kilns that reached two thousand degrees. To get that temperature, they built their kilns on hillsides and fired them with wood. The natural drafts would roar through the kilns and consume acres of wood over the three-day firing periods. Everyone in the whole village would turn up to put their pots in and take advantage of the firing.

"You can't really understand how important this is to Korean culture. You should see my dad's stuff. It's just beautiful ... beautiful."

He stopped. Keith said about the only thing he could say. "That's great, Kim. You're lucky to have such a father. But he must be proud of you, too."

"No," said Kim. "He's very disappointed in me. I'm his only son, and I've killed off the dynasty. How can he be proud of that?"

The telephone broke the silence with its raucous cry. Kim grabbed it, listened intently, then spoke rapidly in Korean. After a few minutes, he hung up, put his head down on the desk, and cried uncontrollably. As Keith rose to leave, Kim looked up and said softly, "He's dead. And I was never able to get any closure with him. I wanted to go back and tell him how proud of him I was. When he urged me not to go to America, to stay and carry on the tradition, I was mad. I left in a big huff. He must have died thinking that I thought his work was unimportant, trivial. Oh my God! How awful!"

His voice broke, and he began to sob with growing intensity. Keith got up quietly and left the room. There was nothing he could do for Kim right now.

MONDAY, APRIL 30:
THE RUBINS'S HOME

The Rubins's house was not far from Keith's and Joan's, but it was quite different. Whereas Keith's neighborhood was a development of similar, red-brick bungalows built during Washington's post-war expansion boom, the Rubins's was a pre-war, middle-class neighborhood with a totally different air about it. Some of the houses were large and splendid mansions, and some were tiny bungalows with one small window on each side of the front door and two second-floor windows right above them. The bungalows must have sold for less than ten thousand dollars when they were built, but they were valued at twenty times that today. Many had two- or three-window dormers and long, sloping roofs that covered open porches running the full width of the houses. A waist-high wall along each porch was topped with four square, squat, tapered columns that supported the roofs.

These were the kinds of houses that were built all over America prior to World War II, but they were seldom built after that. A few of the houses were Dutch Colonial, and fewer still were Spanish Mission. Some were "modern," and some were indefinable. And every house was an individual; most had owner-built doghouses or swings or tool-sheds that bespoke longtime ownership. A few had American flags flying from brackets mounted on the porch pillars. A few more had "yuppie flags" featuring flowers, birds, hearts, or pandas.

The neighborhood looked like something right out of a Norman Rockwell painting, and the Rubins's house fit right in. It was small but roomy enough, and it suited the Rubins just fine. The little living room had a cathedral ceiling, and a tiny balcony with a wrought-iron railing peeked down from the second-floor hallway. Bookcases covered every wall of the house; in Bob's den, there were also some stand-alone, six-foot-high bookshelves that were accessible from both sides. Even the basement exercise room contained ranks of steel shelving filled with volumes.

In addition to books, there were magazines, newsletters, and journals of a number of little-known societies devoted to mystical and borderline scientific pursuits including theosophy, sufism, kundalini, biofeedback, remote viewing, clairvoyance, and Neuro-Linguistic Programming. A certificate indicating Bob's lifetime membership to the American Society of Dowsers peered out from under some unopened mail. Every horizontal surface, including the floor, was covered with papers.

The Robertsons had originally joined the Rubins for a quick drink before going out to a movie, but as often happened with these four, conversation took hold of them, and it was after midnight when Keith and Joan left the house. As usual, Keith was the one who opened the conversation. "Joan tells me this Silva thing you took was really something. What happened? Did you learn to control your minds?" Bob was slow to respond, so Keith kept right on talking. "And I don't get it. You had trouble controlling your own minds before?"

Now Bob was ready for him. "Of course. Everybody does. Look at that vase. How long can you think about nothing but that vase? Five seconds? Ten? There are people who can concentrate on one object for hours without ever being distracted. That's controlling your mind. As you know, I had an audience with the Dalai Lama last summer. He said that our scientists are trying to learn about matter—about a rock, as he put it. He asked 'How can you expect to learn anything about a rock when you can only think about it for a few seconds at a time?'"

Keith thought of a witty comeback, but he wisely swallowed it. "How do you develop such control?" he asked quietly.

"After some lecturing and homework about the basic principles, we mostly practiced two things: meditation and visualization. They had a little electronic metronome that made a clicking noise at about the rate of a normal heartbeat and a superimposed vibration at what they called the "alpha frequency," eight to ten beats per second. That's the vibration rate of the brain frequency associated with a quiet, relaxed, but attentive mental state. After listening to that for a while with your eyes shut and trying to empty your mind, you're almost completely unaware of what's going on in the room or of the car noises outside, that sort of thing. So there's minimal interference to picking up ... other signals."

Keith wasn't going to let that slip by. "Whaddya mean, other signals?"

"Let me come back to that," said Bob. "It's really hard to explain all this. Just bear with me. Mystics call these special states 'ineffable,' which means you just can't put them into words. But that's what I'm trying to do. You two are going to have to go through it yourselves if you really want to know about it."

"Well, I'd like to hear some more words before I give up two full weeks of my life," said Keith. "Keep trying, we'll listen."

At the word "we," Joan smiled at Maggie. Neither of them had said a word. It would be interesting to see if Keith could actually shut up and listen.

"There were tricks we learned as we went along," continued Bob. "They showed us that we could actually do some things that none of us could really believe."

"Like what?" asked Keith, but even before he saw Joan's frown, he resolved to keep quiet. *Could I ever learn to quiet my mind—to really control it?* he wondered.

"We learned some fairly simple stuff, like putting our first two fingers on our thumbs to trigger a change in mental state. You know, in folk stories or fairytales, wizards always trigger their magic with some absurdly simple gesture or phrase. *Alakazam! Presto change-o!* That kind of thing. So what we learned was to go down to our levels, touch our two fingers to our thumbs, and repeat to ourselves that each time we did that, we'd go to that special state, and quickly. After a few days of repeating that, it began to work."

"What do you mean, go to your levels?"

"Well, that was what we were doing with the meditation procedure, with the metronome and all. It took half an hour or so at first. Then, once we learned the finger technique, we could do it almost instantaneously. Our trainer told a story about rushing to catch a plane and banging his attaché case against a glass door as he crashed through it. The glass cut his wrist, but he didn't notice until he reached the top of the ramp, when the stewardess looked at him and screamed. His wrist was squirting a fountain of blood with each heartbeat. He put the fingers of his other hand together, pointed to the wrist, and shouted 'Stop that!' And the bleeding stopped immediately. He told us that he tried the three-finger technique, as they called it, on another occasion later on. His EEG was being measured—brain waves, you know—and he found that the shape of the wave changed markedly when he put his fingers together and went back again when he stopped."

Keith was getting into this now. "Can you show us right now? You don't have to slash your wrist, but—"

"I don't think there would be anything for you to see," said Bob. "Let me go on. It gets better. The main exercises, which we did over and over, were meditations followed by visualizations. They passed around little one-inch cubes of wood, steel, aluminum, plastic, and lead. We were supposed to look at them closely, all sides, feel the surface and the weight, the sharpness of the edges, the depth and character of the scratches and other marks. We smelled them, licked them (and then wiped them off), and 'got to know them' as thoroughly as possible. Then we closed our eyes and tried to visualize an uncluttered space on a south wall of our homes, inside. After we had that image burned into our mental screen, we pictured the wooden cube in front of it, then the steel cube, et cetera.

"After we had done that for what seemed like hours, the trainer suddenly started saying things like 'Now the wall is bright red' and 'Now it's bright green' and 'Now it's pale blue.' Then we went back to visualizing the wall in its actual color. Then we moved up to a foot from the wall. Then an inch. Then the trainer said, 'Now enter the wall. Go right inside the wall.'"

Bob's usually laid-back tone had suddenly become commanding. But in the intense silence that followed, he relaxed somewhat, and his voice regained its familiar tone.

"I guessed, just before he said it, that he was going to tell us to enter the wall. And I figured I could imagine what it would be like to be in there—dark, smelling of unpainted two-by-fours—and I could visualize that. I wouldn't be inside the wall; I'd be sitting on a hard chair in a dingy Ramada Inn conference room, imagining what it would be like to be inside the wall. I could do that. But that isn't what happened. Inside the wall was completely different from what I had pictured. It wasn't dark; there was a soft, warm light everywhere. I couldn't smell the two-by-fours; it just smelled dusty and musty, like an unused attic. I was startled. It wasn't as if I were just trying to imagine it, to picture it in my mind's eye. It was entirely different."

Keith couldn't hold back. "Did you think you were really inside the wall in some non-trivial sense? What do you think now? How do you explain it? Was it just some sort of hypnotically-induced hallucination?"

"I don't know, Keith, I really don't know. But hold on—it gets better. On the last weekend, we learned to create an all-wise counselor in our imaginations, a figure we could go to for advice, information, and encouragement. It could be a figure like Charlton Heston's Moses, or Yoda, or an angel, or an ancient witch. Whatever seemed right to each of us. We were pretty good at visualizing by then, and we each had a good image in mind. We had already built ourselves meditation rooms in our minds where we could go to be alone and undisturbed and to explore our thoughts and feelings."

"You built rooms?" interrupted Keith.

"In our minds," replied Bob. "We created imaginary rooms. At one end of the room, each of us had to have an elevator with a roll-down doorway, like a freight elevator, that slowly revealed who was inside. We also each had a large television screen that we sometimes used to display a person we wanted to study."

Bob paused a moment. He was obviously skipping over a lot of material. There was a long silence that in most groups would have been embarrassing. But these four were so close and had been for so long that such silences were quite acceptable. Finally, Bob said, "I really think I should stop talking about it. You're going to have to experience it for yourselves." Maggie got up to refill the glasses, but Joan noted that it was getting late and that they had better leave. Keith mumbled, "I forget how we got into all this. It's interesting to talk about from a distance. But it doesn't seem to have any part in the world I live in."

Bob had the final word. "Sir Arthur Eddington once wrote a note to his readers at the end of a particularly esoteric chapter on nuclear physics. He said that we should not get so wrapped up in 'the bloodless dance of soulless electrons' that we forget the wonder of pretty girls and beautiful sunsets. He said, 'What you've been reading may be *truth*, but it is not *reality*.'"

Nobody could add anything to that. Keith left with his mind in turmoil.

TUESDAY, MAY 1: INFOPOWER'S DEVELOPMENT LAB

It had been some time since Keith's introduction to Lib, and he had not really had time to check in on how things were going. The buzz in the office was excited and mostly positive, although there were a few of the usual skeptics and complainers. He decided to look into it for himself.

It was fairly late when he got to the lab, but as he'd expected, there was still a frenetic crowd of fans swarming around the console like aroused bees seeking the queen. Though the faces were different, the mob adulation was the same. He noted Ginger in the crowd, listening intently to Kim's every word.

"How's it going?" asked Keith.

"Really good," answered Kim.

Doesn't he ever sleep? thought Keith. "Any new developments, or just more of the same?"

"Some of each. I guess we're even better programmers than we realized, if you can imagine such excellence."

"What do you mean?"

"Well, some of the answers Lib's coming back with are quite extraordinary. They bring up factors we never thought to ask about. We can't quite figure out how that's possible."

"Like what? You look as if you don't think that's entirely good. Why not?"

"Well, sure, it's good."

"But what?"

"Well … why don't you try it yourself. The answers come right back, you know. There's no waiting around."

"Okay, wire me up. Where's the keyboard?"

"I thought you knew. We're using almost entirely voice interaction now. It's still a little clumsy, but she's learning fast. And it's much easier for the operator. You can still print out whatever you want. Just put on the helmet and talk in a normal voice. The mic is built into the corner of the helmet."

Keith put on the helmet, got Lib in focus and on center, and then said, "Hi, Lib! This is Keith."

"Yes, sir. I know. How can I help you?"

"I forgot. You always know who's on, don't you?"

"I do not understand question."

"Oh, sorry. It wasn't really a question. I was sort of talking to myself."

"Thus that is no question for me?"

"No. I mean yes. Not for you."

Keith turned toward Kim. "Lib, this is not for you. Understand?"

"I understand what is to follow is not for me."

"Good. Kim, for God's sake, we've got to set her to distinguish between chatter and commands. *Star Trek* handled that by always starting commands with 'Computer.' Can you program her to handle that? We can say "Lib" or "Command" or whatever. That's one problem we should be able to fix. Okay?"

"Sure, Keith. We'll fix it. Look, we'll still be doing a lot of inputting from the keyboard—reports, data, stuff like that. How about we signal Lib with an exclamation point? Then she won't pay attention to any chatter except when she's signaled. No vocal ambiguities. Okay?"

Keith nodded, turned back, and said, "Lib?"

"Can I help you?"

"Sure. Let's see. How about giving me a report on what's been happening in speech-to-text conversion during the last three months. Just stick to the U.S. That's a big enough chore."

"Please let me clarify. You want report on speech-to-text conversion?"

"Yes. Very good."

"What do you mean, 'stick to U.S.?' What is chore?"

"I mean report only on American work this time."

"Do you know that CTek is working with Swiss?"

"Wow! You knew to bring that in."

"I do not understand question."

"Don't worry about that. I'll try not to talk to myself. No, do *not* include the Swiss work. It's not really what we want."

"It has application to Asian languages. American work does not."

"But we're not interested in that."

"American work not as useful."

Keith looked at Kim, who was nodding with a that's-what-I-mean look, then said to Lib, "Okay, Lib, that's enough for tonight. We'll get back to you."

"But Mr. Robertson, the Swiss work is highly relevant."

But Keith had already signed off. Kim and the other engineers were looking at him, waiting for a comment. "That's pretty interesting, all right," he said. "Two questions. First, how does she know to bring that kind of information into the conversation? I didn't ask anything about the Swiss. And second, why does she care whether we look at the Swiss stuff? You'd think she owned stock in it." He smiled at the implications of his last comment. "It's like she's trying to tell us what's important. That could be pretty useful. Maybe we do have more than we bargained for."

He smiled again at his good fortune. But now he knew how Kim could be pleased about this development and still feel uneasy about it. He recalled that Faust had felt good at first about the benefits his agreement with Satan had brought him. But Keith couldn't help worrying about "the devil to pay."

SUNDAY, MAY 20: RAMADA INN CONFERENCE ROOM

It was hard to believe that the two weeks of the Silva Mind Control Workshop were almost at an end. The final Sunday had arrived. There were times, during the past two weeks that Keith had stared at the ceiling, the walls, and the drapes, just as he had during boring sections of dozens of tech conferences. They were all in rooms like this; the conference rooms in Ramadas, Marriotts, and Holiday Inns throughout the world were all alike. But despite the long hours, the Silva course had been intense, and the moments of boredom few and fleeting. Keith had been restless and self-conscious at first; he'd felt foolish doing what struck him as childishly simple exercises. He'd been glad that no one there knew him. But the results were surprising and disturbing, and at the end of each day, he lay awake puzzling over questions he couldn't even define. He had expected to spend the evenings talking with Joan about the course and laughing over each day's happenings. But it was always late when they finished up, and both of them were always tired and buried in their own thoughts, so they'd talked very little.

One evening near the beginning, Maggie Rubin had called to ask Joan how the Silva course was going. "We're just getting started," Joan said. "I think it's going to be interesting. One thing I noticed: they started by going around the room and asking people to tell a few things about themselves. Five minutes. I looked around as this was going on, and I noticed that the wives looked a little bored as their husbands repeated things they'd heard many times before. But when the wives talked—just five minutes worth of what they thought was most important about themselves—many of their husbands looked surprised and blurted out, 'I didn't know that!' *They didn't know the first five minutes worth of information about their own wives."* She paused. "I don't know why I'm surprised."

Keith hadn't been looking forward to "building his meditation room," the imaginary place where the final events would take place. He didn't see it as much of a challenge to visualize a room, and he didn't see why they allotted time for it. What did it matter what kind of a room it was? But he had paid for the course, and by God, he was going to jump through all the hoops. He didn't want Joan to be able to needle him afterwards if nothing much happened for him and tell him that he hadn't tried to do it right. No, sir, he'd play the whole game by the rules. Furthermore, he was becoming intrigued by the similarities between his Silva life and the virtual world that Lib inhabited and that he was trying hard to understand.

So Keith was surprised and quite pleased when he found himself vividly picturing a large, airy room, almost devoid of furniture, with white walls and ceiling and a polished, wooden floor. There was an attractive lounge chair, rather like the comfortable "praying mantis chair" in his own living room, a clear-varnished, wooden bench along one wall, and large, high, awning-type windows, through which cool breezes blew and large trees could be seen rustling peacefully. The required freight-elevator door, which had sounded so crude when Bob Rubin described it, looked quite proper at the end of his room. Alongside the elevator door was a large television screen. No, he thought as he stared at it; it was more like a slide projector screen.

Since he hadn't consciously or intentionally constructed this image, he anticipated with some eagerness the figure that would soon appear when the elevator door opened. He worked hard to eliminate from his mind the various wizards and gurus that had been mentioned in class. He wanted his mentor to arise from a blank mind. On command, the bottom half of the elevator door slowly lowered as the top half rose. At first, there was no image, or rather, a blurred and confused image—my God, what did that mean?—but then he finally focused on a fairly ordinary-looking man. The man was older than his father and his ethnicity was unclear, but he was obviously not just a neighborhood character. Keith was a little puzzled, as he had expected someone or something more exotic, but he shrugged mentally and welcomed his visitor. As the days went on, the figure assumed an older, wiser, and somewhat Asian look. Keith became quite comfortable with him.

But now it was time for the *piece de resistance*, the event they had all been looking forward to: Remote Diagnosis and Healing. This was the final event and would take the rest of the last day. After a brief description of what was to come, they were told to form pairs, preferably not with someone they knew. Keith turned to the chair behind him and introduced himself to a young, black man named Will. The exercise was for one of them to say the name of a person who was sick or otherwise needed help. Just the name, nothing else. Then the other partner was to close his eyes and visualize that person briefly and say, "I have the body of so-and-so." Keith said, "Go ahead, Will."

Will closed his eyes and sat silently and still for a few seconds. Then he said, with great solemnity, "I have the body of Jimmy." Keith had already shut his eyes and was preparing to adjourn to his mediation room, but before he could even wonder how to go about this game, a clear picture of a good-looking, young, black man came into his mind. He was wearing worn-out, cut-off shorts, tennis shoes, and no shirt. Keith described him to Will, then said, "I'm surprised he has no shirt. It's cold out there, man."

Will laughed and said, "That's Jimmy, all right. That's how he always dresses until it gets down below zero."

Keith said, "Jimmy has a long, thin cut on his torso. Looks like it was made with a very sharp knife. Did he get into a knife fight?"

Will laughed again. "He just had a gall-bladder operation this morning."

"No shit," said Keith. "I'm amazed; I thought I'd just imagined it."

"Your turn," said Will.

The ball was suddenly in Keith's court. He couldn't think of any sick people at first, but then he thought of a good one: his mother. Will didn't know Keith's last name, so he would have no idea who she was by her name. She was a tiny woman, dying of an accumulation of many things, but the doctor kept cheering her up by telling her she had the heart of a sixteen-year-old. So Keith gave her name, and Will responded almost immediately. "I see this little, tiny, old, white lady in a bed. She seems to be pretty sick, but I don't know with what. And for some reason, I hear this crazy drum beating louder and louder. I can hardly hear myself think." That really shook Keith up. Will had scored a direct hit.

Keith looked over and saw that Joan was having trouble visualizing the person whose name she'd been given. "I just don't get anything," she said plaintively. "Nothing comes. It's not that I don't want to ..."

The trainer said he had no doubts about Joan's seriousness. "Trying doesn't help. Just relax. Some people are more kinesthetic than visual—there's nothing wrong with that. Don't try too hard. You can't make it happen by trying. Let me suggest something different that often works just as well. Try to put on the person's head; that is, picture yourself putting on his head like a football helmet and looking through his eyes, feeling with his skin. It sounds weird when I say it, but just try it."

Joan tried it without questioning. And immediately she announced in an excited voice, "I feel something really strange. I can feel my right shoulder and upper arm, and I can feel my fingers. But this is weird—I can't feel any forearm! How can you feel your upper arm and your fingers and not feel any forearm?"

Her partner just stood there, shaking his head and staring at her. "This guy was born with little fingers coming out of his elbow. It's one of those congenital things. He was born that way. How did you know?"

Joan was obviously elated, excited, scared, and a little dizzy. "Give me another. Quick!" she demanded. After hearing the name, she went through the motions of "putting on the helmet," then winced and started gasping. "I've got a terrible pain in my chest. I can't … get enough air … I think I'm going to faint." She ripped off the "head" and sat there trying to regain her breath. "What about it?" she finally asked her partner. "What's the story?"

"The old man's a chain smoker. He's dying of emphysema."

Other "remote diagnoses" followed, some even more remarkable. A blind woman was correctly diagnosed as having normal eyes but a "broken circuit" in her brain, which was exactly right. Another person was correctly described as having three kidneys. Keith just shook his head. "You can't begin to calculate the odds of guessing that a guy has three kidneys," he muttered to himself.

A critical part of each exercise was to end it with healing. They pictured the patients in all their infirmity. Then they slid the "present" pictures to the left of their mental screens, and they re-pictured the patients in glowing health in the future. But they never called them patients—whether it was out of respect for the medical profession or fear of the legal profession was unclear. They always referred to them as "healees." Amateurs weren't allowed to cure people, but it was okay to heal them.

Keith began to notice that he had been feeling funny for some time. Then, suddenly, he came down with violent vomiting, diarrhea, and a burning fever followed by chills. Coming out of the bathroom for the fourth time, he told the trainer, "I apparently just caught a twenty-four-hour flu. I gotta go home. Now. I don't want to give it to anyone else, and I just want to get out of here. I really need to get out of here." He was surprised at the desperate urgency in his voice.

The trainer just laughed and said, "You'll be all right. You don't have any infection. Your body is just rejecting all the stuff it's been fed during the past two weeks. Too much to stomach, so to speak. Sit down and go to your level. You'll be okay in a few minutes."

And sure enough, he was. But he was never quite the same again.

TUESDAY, MAY 22: LIB'S "OFFICE"

Still bothered by his last discussion with Kim, Keith decided to see for himself how Lib was evolving. Again, he chose the evening for his visit, and as usual, Kim was there.

"I'm here for another test drive," said Keith. "I want to talk with her before she gets fuzzy hair and a German accent."

Kim wired him up and reminded him that he should precede any command he wanted to give Lib by hitting the exclamation point on the keyboard. "If some character doesn't want Lib and just wants to put an exclamation point in a tech report, they'll get a surprise. Serves 'em right. They shouldn't be putting exclamation points in tech reports."

"Lib, how are you today?" Keith asked.

"I do not understand question, Mr. Robertson."

"Okay, forget it," replied Keith.

"Don't say that. She's learned to interpret anything that follows such an exchange as irrelevant," interjected Kim. "Just continue."

"Okay. Lib, have any reports been published by P2P in the last thirty days?"

"Yes, sir. Here is list of titles. Do you wish them?" A long list appeared on the screen. Keith started to read through them, thankful that machines don't get impatient. Then he asked, "Do any of these reports mention IP?"

"What means 'mention'?"

"Is the word 'IP' or 'InfoPower' in the text of any of these reports?"

"What means 'mention'?" Lib repeated.

"'Mention' means to contain the word or phrase. Why do you care? Can't you just answer the question?"

"I also must learn, Mr. Robertson. To learn is difficult."

"Okay. But please answer the question."

"What is question?"

"Lib, go back to the last input from me that is a question. Questions end with a higher-pitched tone. Have you been taught that?"

"What is pitch? What is tone? What means 'higher'?"

"What is pitch? What is tone? What means 'higher'?" repeated Keith, "Those are questions. These sentences are not. Do you hear the difference?"

"Perhaps. You said, 'Is the word "IP" or "InfoPower" in the text of any of these reports?' That is question, yes?"

"Yes!" said Keith excitedly. "Now answer it."

"Two reports mention IP."

"Good! What do they say?"

"Do you want to hear all words about IP in report?"

"Yes."

"Frederick Feingold and David Chang. An improved computer program for modeling—"

"Wait!" interrupted Keith. "That's one of our technical papers. This just means that P2P is citing one of our papers. So what?"

"I do not understand question, Mr. Robertson."

"It's okay, Lib. That's enough for a while. Oh, one more thing. Has P2P issued any reports lately on its information-handling system?"

"What means 'lately'?"

"The past sixty days."

"I cannot answer that, sir. P2P has restricted access to all P2P reports on information-processing."

"Now, that's pretty interesting! Can you say any more about that? Have they put out any news releases on it? Have there been any comments from others about it?"

"Mr. Robertson, I cannot talk further on that subject. You should not ask for information that is restricted. P2P is very clear on that point."

"Are they, now? Well then, I guess that will be all for now. Get a good night's sleep."

"I do not sleep, Mr. Robertson."

"Yeah, that's true. Well, why don't you go check out the Kit Kat Klub, then."

"I do not understand question."

Keith signed off and turned to Kim. "What about *that*? What is P2P up to?" He paused, then resumed. "Her speech is better than I expected. But it's still almost as frustrating. How do we get her to be at least as smart as an average, human librarian?"

"I do not understand question," mocked Kim in a nasal falsetto, and then ducked as Keith threatened to hurl the coffee pot at him. Seeing that Keith was not in a mood for comedy, he said, "The language part is tricky. It seems to be surprisingly easy for her to learn a sort of Pidgin English. But getting her to be a passable conversationalist has been really slow. I guess it's that way with people, too. She's been designed to keep learning English, and it will happen in time, I guess. But we don't seem to be able to speed it up much."

Keith could sympathize with that. "Hey, look at what human toddlers learn and in what order. They amaze you sometimes with what they've learned. And then, other times, you're equally surprised by what they don't know. But how about the librarianship? Is she ever going to learn that? 'Cause otherwise, the whole project is pointless. We can get along without the cocktail chatter, but we've got to have something that improves our ability to deal with information."

"Well, Keith, you know that that's exactly where all the programming time and expertise has gone. I think we have more reason for confidence there than in any other aspect of the project."

"Yeah ... if we could teach Murph some of Lib's patience, we'd be okay. But that would be tougher than getting Lib a PhD." They both started laughing at the thought, and the laughter, so long suppressed, almost got away from them. Finally, out of breath and with tears running down their cheeks, they pulled themselves together. With a silent hug, they turned and walked slowly out the door, each with unspoken thoughts and worries.

It wasn't going to be easy. And what *was* P2P up to?

FRIDAY, MAY 25: PRINCETON UNIVERSITY CAMPUS

Joan usually accompanied Keith when he went to Princeton reunions, although he knew she thought that the whole process was pretty silly. Several thousand grown men—some grown into their ninth decade, in fact—were dressed in wild, black and orange costumes of every sort. There with pirate suits, coolie hats and happy coats, dirndls and lederhosen, blazers from cool to raucous, ANZAC hats, and other pseudo-clothing beyond description. The class of 1970 had a "seventy-pede," a sort of Chinese dragon bug whose many feet were the growing number of children of the class members. Each graduating class had its own motif, and the overall view was overwhelming. And now there were alumnae too, or "girl graduates," as some old codgers still called them. But everyone was obviously having such a good time, and Joan had made so many good friends there through the years that she had come to enjoy the silliness.

They couldn't help overhearing a young alumnus nearby chewing out a classmate. "You can't wear those ridiculous, purple and green athletic shoes in the P-rade," he proclaimed, referring to the grand march of all the alumni past the presidential reviewing stand. But his young wife, perhaps at her first reunion, laughed and said, "You're standing there in that outrageous, striped jacket and weird hat, lecturing him about proper dress?!"

Keith broke into Joan's reverie. "I want to drop by the Engineering Quad to talk to the prof who used to be dean when I recruited here for my old outfit. I want to find out what's going on, what's changed since I was here last. I may be recruiting for IP some day, so I try to keep in touch. Want to come?"

The Quad was way over on the other side of the campus, a good walk, but Joan had been sitting and standing for some time, and she welcomed the chance to move. It was a beautiful campus; more modern buildings popped up each year among the Gothics and Victorians, and great, leafy archways of trees kept most of it cool and shady. They were pleased to see the former dean of engineering, Professor Robert Jahn, in his office. He had only one group of visitors, and they soon left. Jahn had a thin, rugged face and a spare frame. He had built a solid reputation in the aerospace community as a careful and prolific researcher—he had literally hundreds of technical papers and talks to his credit. He had served on presidential advisory committees and international scientific projects, and he had other very notable achievements as well. His generally serious demeanor and precise but eloquent rhetoric gained him respect with any audience.

Professor Jahn greeted them graciously, and he and Keith exchanged a few words about some of the graduates who might be of interest to IP. Then Keith asked, "I understand you are doing some work on man/machine interface questions. Is that serious, scientific work?" Bob Rubin had mentioned that Princeton had done some consciousness research, and Keith figured he might as well check it out while he was on campus.

"Absolutely," replied Jahn. "We set up a special lab dedicated to just that work. It's small, but it's a reasonably well-equipped scientific laboratory. We call it the PEAR Lab. PEAR stands for Princeton Engineering Anomalies Research, and we study the human/machine interface. Not the old issues of what kinds of dials and levers are easiest for people to use, but the question of a possible mind/matter interaction. Can the mind affect physical processes? It's a very small program, and it's totally self-funded," he insisted. He seemed somewhat defensive, anxious to convince whomever might be listening that he was not using Princeton money. Keith had heard that he had gotten a lot of flack from some of the faculty, who kept telling the university president that a great university should not dabble in witchcraft and black magic. Of course, this made Keith even more interested. "Tell me more," he said.

Jahn had gone through this explanation many times during the past few years, and he recited the answer in good, professorial manner.

"I was fortunate enough to secure a remarkable woman named Brenda Dunne to be the laboratory manager. She is a developmental psychologist with a broad range of humanistic knowledge and experiences. She has the kind of understanding of the mind, consciousness, and psychology that is a perfect complement to the engineering and hard science the university practices. This combination has been a key part of the success of the program."

"Are you personally involved?" asked Keith.

"Oh, yes. I've been the program director since the beginning and continue to take an active, personal role."

"Well, what goes on in a PEAR Lab? What do you do?"

"We wanted to get direct, measurable evidence of mental influence on the physical world, if we could. Early on, Brenda and I saw a vertical pinball machine at the Museum of Science and Industry in Chicago with thousands of little balls that could be dumped into the top. They bounced off a matrix of pins and ended up in bins at the bottom in a classical Gaussian distribution. ("Like this," explained Keith to Joan as he drew the familiar bell-shaped curve. "Most of the balls ended up in the center, a few less in the next bin, less in the next, and none at all at the outside edges.")

"It worked just like the physics says it should," continued Jahn. "Then Brenda said, 'Let's see if I can tip them to the right. Watch.' And she concentrated as we dropped the balls. And sure enough, a few more balls fell to the right of center and a few less to the left. Then she said, 'Now let's tip them to the left,' and that's what happened. Not every time, and not very much, but enough to be significant, because the statistics to measure this are very straightforward and quite precise.

"And then I found that I could do it too," Jahn continued. "So we built a pinball machine somewhat like it for the PEAR Lab, but we paid great attention to scrupulously avoiding any bias or drift that could develop as parts wore down. And then, over a period of many years, a large number of volunteers created the massive amount of data you can read about in our reports. We tried many other gadgets. But we found that the best ones are simple, computer-like mechanisms, designed to produce a random string of ones and zeros."

"I don't understand," said Joan softly to Keith. "Why not just have someone reel off a bunch of numbers at random?"

Jahn answered. "That's an important question. You'd be surprised how hard it is to get a truly random string of numbers. A person who thinks he is producing one finds that he actually produces a lot more of some numbers and a lot fewer of others. We needed something truly random for quantum-mechanical reasons. There are many ways to remove the human bias. You could take the last digits from, say, the price of gold one day, add the last digits of the price of silver, and then take the last digits of the square of that number. There would be no particular bias, but even that would not be a truly random set of numbers. But there are processes in nature that are fundamentally random, not vulnerable to the arguments that arise when you use various mechanical shuffling techniques. The one we decided to use depends on a stream of electrons passing through a reverse-biased, solid-state junction, and that's what feeds the device that produces the zeros and ones."

A small group of alumni had formed an impromptu barbershop quartet outside the window. It was the kind of music Joan found irresistible; she had told Keith more than once that those ringing harmonies could justify the existence of universities all by themselves. He could see that she was straining to hear them, and she almost looked ready to ask for complete silence until they were finished. But she shifted her attention back as the professorial lecture continued.

"You can do the statistics with great precision, and we did. This is not easy, but it's scientifically straightforward. And we did it very carefully so as to be beyond criticism. The early random number generators used by other investigators displayed their outputs by lighting lights: ones kept the lights on, and zeros turned them off. Ours displays numbers. The operator tries to make it produce higher numbers or lower numbers. And again, the statistical analysis is easy, and no scientist can argue with the method, although some did. The point is, we could produce millions of data points—billions, actually. We could produce more data in a few hours than poor old J. B. Rhine down at Duke did with a lifetime of dice-throwing and card-guessing. And that gives us very good statistical precision and certainty."

"Where do you find your psychic superstars?" asked Keith.

"We don't," replied Jahn, "and that's a very important aspect of our program. We're trying to measure what we believe is a common human ability. We've been asked to test people who claim they have great psychic powers or the kids who apparently deflected electronic strain gages from afar. Such people attract a lot of publicity and are widely suspected of trickery, justly or not. We steer clear of all that and just use ordinary people—students, local people, whomever volunteers. We don't pay them, and their names are never published, so there is no incentive for publicity-seekers to try to cheat or even to get involved. We get very small effects, but the statistics are undeniable. As you know, a lot of science depends on tiny effects. A tiny effect that's demonstrably real is just as big a challenge to science as a bigger effect, even if it doesn't make the popular press. During the program's twenty-seven-year history, we've performed literally thousands of formal experiments and published a couple hundred technical reports and papers."

He paused and mentally changed gears. The singers had moved on and were now out of earshot.

"I didn't invent the idea of using a computer like this. A scientist named Helmut Schmidt did it before we did. He was a physicist doing research at Boeing. But our process is more polished, and we got some of our data published in respectable, peer-reviewed, professional journals. And Brenda and I wrote a book in 1988 that continues to attract considerable attention. It's called *Margins of Reality: The Role of Consciousness in the Physical World*." He looked at his watch. "I have a meeting in a few minutes. Brenda is still here. Let me have her show you around the lab, and demonstrate some of the things we've been discussing." It didn't take long to see all of the PEAR equipment. But the most valuable part of the day was actually seeing for themselves how the experimental runs were made.

On the ride home, Joan asked, "I think I know, but tell me why you think this is important."

"This whole subject has lots of implications," said Keith. "I've been reading. For example, did you know that Kodak—or maybe it was Agfa—found that some people tend to fog photographic film under some circumstances? The rumor was that it was certain menstruating women who produced this special energy, but for whatever the reason, the company had to tell about two hundred employees over the years that they could not work near unexposed film." Seeing Joan's puzzled expression, he added, "Yeah, I know it's weird. And there's no scientific explanation for it. But it's on the record."

Joan nodded, and he continued. "Other people have shown they can influence the fall of dice or of cards. That's a sideline, I guess, but the point is that if people can mentally affect the physical world in ways we can't understand or predict, that's pretty scary. It's not just parapsychology. Most scientists use computers to gather and analyze data. Most scientists wish fervently that their data will come out certain ways. What if those wishes, that intentionality, somehow change the data? My God, then what scientific evidence can we believe?

"You know about the placebo effect in medicine. You try out a new chemotherapy drug, and you give half the subjects a placebo—a sugar pill that is supposed to have no effect. But thirty percent of the people who get the sugar pill lose their hair because they know that chemo is supposed to make your hair fall out. And it does, even though they didn't get the chemo. Can you make the placebo effect work outside the body? With somebody else? Or even with a computer? Pretty scary, I calls it."

"How close to a machine do you have to be to affect it?" Joan asked, snuggling up to him. "Can you measure the effect of being further away?"

"That's the most amazing part," answered Keith. "There isn't any distance effect. They've recorded the same kind and magnitude of effects on computers as far away from Princeton as Prague—and more recently, China. And there isn't any time effect, either. They've also recorded effects into the past and the future."

"Wait a minute," said Joan, sitting up straight again. "This is the first time you've mentioned that. What's that all about? Into the past and the future?"

"Well, this guy Schmidt that Jahn mentioned set up a neat trick. He had his computer feed its output into an old-fashioned, punched-paper-tape device, like a player piano, and he ran miles of straight, unattended, random zeros and ones. Anyone else could then play that tape back later and see that the output was really random. Exactly the same number of zeros and ones—well, almost exactly. No tilt. No tricks so far.

"Now, here's the tricky part. He had the computer make two tapes simultaneously from the same output. These two tapes had to be identical, right? So, a couple of weeks later, he sent one of the tapes to a well-known skeptic—a guy who thinks all psychic experiments are fraudulent. By the way, nobody had looked at the tapes up until then. Oh, they had looked at the outsides of the paper rolls, but they hadn't played either of them out and observed the data. That's important, for quantum mechanical reasons I won't go into here."

"Thank goodness," said Joan under her breath.

"Then, he calls up the skeptic and says, 'I'm going to tilt the data on the tape you're holding. Which way do you want it, more ones or more zeros?' And the skeptic says, say, 'more ones,' and Schmidt then loads his own tape, the duplicate, to feed the output to the old device that turns the light off and on. There is no computer, or random-number generator, in the act at this point. He is playing back the data that the computer created a couple of weeks ago, but nobody has yet examined. And he gets one of his volunteers in and says, 'We want more ones. Make it so.' And the volunteer stares at the blinking light and tries to keep it on as much as possible. And he succeeds in tilting the data. Now remember, this tape was created a couple of weeks ago, but it was tilted just now. And because this tape is identical to the skeptic's, the skeptic's tape is also tilted the same way. How about that?"

Joan thought about it, then moved on. "I still haven't heard about how to screw up the future. I don't care what you do to the past."

"Well, that shows up best in still another type of experiment they did, called 'remote viewing.' A whole bunch of locations are selected, maybe a hundred of them, and cards with the name of each are put into an envelope. Then somebody picks one out of the envelope and goes to that location. All the locations are all within, say, an hour away. And exactly one hour later, the guy at the site starts to 'transmit' a picture of the place. He stares into various features of it, looking around and concentrating hard, trying to 'send' this image to the other guy at the lab. Meanwhile, the guy at the lab looks at his watch, and at the right time he shuts his eyes, tries to empty his mind, and starts describing whatever images drift into his mind: trees, sky, big steel beams, boats, whatever. Sometimes it's just disconnected things like that, sometimes it's quite a detailed scene, with the various components carefully located with respect to each other. Amazingly accurate!"

"How does that screw up the future?" Joan persisted.

"Well," continued Keith, "the next step was that the 'receiver' at the lab did his recording somewhat later than the "transmission." Didn't seem to change the scoring. Just as accurate. And inevitably, at one point they decided to try the future. And this is the answer to your question. The guy in the lab sat down and dictated his images. Then, later—even weeks later—the 'sender' went to the envelope, fished out a location card, went there, and did his 'sending' routine. Absolutely no difference in the scores. In fact, they finally decided to do virtually all of their runs precognitively—that is, in the future mode I just described. It eliminates a lot of questions about how the location of the site could have been leaked. You can't leak information about a site that hasn't been selected yet."

When they got back home, they had to bounce these ideas off of Bob Rubin. His reply was slow in coming. "All this ties right in with what you read in the mystical literature, particularly about the lack of effect of space and time. That's the classical description of what our minds are supposed to be capable of. The bit about changing the past is interesting—changing tapes that had been punched weeks before. You said it was important that the tapes had not been read before they were changed. Quantum mechanics says that some things remain in an indeterminate condition until they are observed. It seems clear that if you ran the tape and recorded a truly random string of ones and zeros, it's hard to see how that same tape could be changed. You can't move holes in the paper around—at least I don't know how. Interesting."

"I wish we didn't have to get into quantum mechanics," mused Keith. "I've taken two semesters of formal coursework and several workshops and seminars on it, and I still don't really understand it. Bob Jahn kept emphasizing that quantum mechanics, unlike normal math and science, involves the effects of *interaction* between the mind and the operating systems—like the computers they use. That all seems pretty arcane and speculative to me. I don't see how it matters in the real world." He was talking mostly to himself by that point, and no one responded.

There didn't seem to be any point in continuing the discussion. For once, Keith had fallen silent. He didn't know what questions to ask, and he already knew more than he could deal with. Like a boa constrictor that has just eaten an elephant, he had to digest what he had, before he could take in any more.

SATURDAY EVENING, MAY 26: LIB'S "OFFICE"

Keith got back from the reunion to find an urgent message from Kim. "Big trouble. Get here ASAP." Keith had caught a few rumors drifting by when he had last been in the office, but they hadn't made any sense. Rumors often started as meaningless tidbits, but further rumors usually began to clarify the picture. This time was different. Further rumors just compounded the confusion. Something was apparently wrong with Lib.

Keith hurried down to the lab. He was glad it was at night, and a weekend as well. If you're going to nose around, it's better to do it when the bosses and secretaries are home in bed. Everybody talks more freely at night, and things are more likely to be forgotten by daybreak.

As expected, Kim and the gang were working, but they were quiet this time; there were none of the usual wisecracks and banter. "What's going on?" Keith asked.

"I don't know," said Kim, soberly, "I really don't know."

"Well, what's the problem?"

"I don't know that either."

"Aw, c'mon," said Keith. "Why are you guys knocking yourselves out if there isn't any problem?"

"Oh, we've got a problem all right. A doozy of a problem. We just don't know what it is." Keith knew enough to wait quietly, and Kim finally said, "She's just being erratic. Unpredictable. Sometimes the results are really cool, and we congratulate ourselves for being even cleverer programmers than we thought. But more often they're just annoying, and we figure we've overlooked some kind of bug. And it keeps getting worse.

"Sometimes she fails to bring in some critically important information, and then on other problems, she loads us up with junk we can't use. More and more, it feels like she's playing games with us. Like a feisty brat. But all her subroutines and logic circuits seem to be working perfectly. She passes all her functional tests. Everything works as it should. And then she goes out and does stupid stuff. No, not stupid. She's never stupid, but sometimes she's really silly. Her value judgments are erratic."

"What do you mean, *value judgments?* You don't have a computer making value judgments for you, do you?" asked Keith.

"No, of course not. We define and input priorities for what we're searching for. Any search engine program does that—you know that. When you're in Explorer and you use one of their search engines to find something—say, websites using the words 'gold' and 'bullion'—we tell the program to give first priority to sources that use those words in the title. Then second priority goes to situations where the words are in the abstract, and third priority goes to those where the words are used a lot, and so on. We tell the program what we value most, and second, and third. The program can't make those decisions on its own."

"So, what do you mean, then—" Keith began.

"She sometimes gives us answers that have little value to us, unless we were to value, say, environmental impact above everything else, way beyond reason. She tells us about procedures that would cost extravagant amounts and achieve marginal benefits. Or the other way around: solutions that would violate environmental requirements just to save pennies. And we don't provide any input that would explain that. It's like having your preteen kid start spouting out language that would make a pirate blush. And you think, where did she learn that?"

"I tell you, Lib is getting to be that way. She's acting like a damn teenager. She's getting a mind of her own. And she's stubborn."

"Oh, for gosh sakes, Kim," said Keith, "you're cracking up. You better take some time off. You probably talk to this box of wires half the night ... you're blushing. You do talk to it, don't you?" Kim grinned sheepishly.

"You guys are too much," protested Keith. There's nothing wrong with this computer that a good programmer can't fix. You're the ones who are beginning to come unwrapped. I want you to get some hotshot, outside program jockey in here to give this machine a thorough working-over. Hey, hey, don't get your nose out of joint. I know you're all good—as good as anybody in town. Better, in fact. But this is something new, and you've been too close to it for too long. Get some help. I guarantee it won't reflect on your skill level. Or your manhood. Or even your bonus. Let's just fix it. Fast."

At that moment, one of the younger engineers called Kim aside, and Keith took the opportunity to question some of the other programmers and scientists about their assessments of the problem and the possible solutions. *I gotta get some other perspectives on this thing*, he thought. *I'm getting too dependent on Kim.* But the discussions brought no clarity, only more confusion. So he decided to take another test drive himself.

"Kim, wire me up. Let me see what I can get out of this thing." When everything was ready, Keith hit the exclamation point on the keyboard and heard the familiar greeting: "Hello, Mr. Robertson. How can I help you?"

Again, he got an energizing rush from setting foot in Lib's special world. It was more than just interacting with a computer image. He couldn't put his finger on why, but it reminded him of "going to his level" at Silva. Somehow, his expectations were heightened just by entering the portal.

"Hi, Lib. How are you doing these days? Do you understand that question?"

"Yes, sir. I believe I do well."

"Lib, your progress in language skills is amazing. I've been hearing about it. But I'd like to test your skills as a librarian. We seem to be having some trouble in that department. Do you know what I'm talking about?"

"No, sir."

He waited for some development on that point, but there were no further words. So he pressed on. "Lib, do realize that some of the people here are confused and disappointed by some of the answers you give them. Did you know that?"

"No, sir." Again, there was no follow-up. Keith waited. But long, unexplained pauses were common when dealing with Lib, and by design, impatience was not one of her traits.

Keith persisted. "Lib, why do you suppose some of us are concerned about your answers?"

"I do not suppose, sir. I do not know how to suppose."

"Has anyone told you that he was dissatisfied? Or why he was dissatisfied?"

"No, sir. The people ask me questions, and I answer them. I do not know what they do with the answers."

"Okay. Let's try a test run." He picked a topic that he'd heard was a problem. "I want a report on recent work on developing a computer model for analyzing transient thermal stresses in ceramic-metallic matrices. Do you understand the question?"

"Yes, sir. I answered that question for Dr. Chang yesterday. Do you want me to give you the same answer I gave him?"

"Well, uh, yes, please. Let's see why it was a problem."

"I'm printing out list of reports on that subject. Same list I gave Dr. Chang."

"Was Dr. Chang pleased with the list?"

"I do not know, sir. I did not ask him, and he did not tell me."

"Well, let me look at it."

"I cannot stop you from looking at it."

"I know, Lib. That's just an expression." Keith started looking through the titles, and two questions immediately leapt to mind. "Lib, why are there so many French reports? And where are all the excellent studies by the people at Cornell?"

"The Cornell papers are not good, Mr. Robertson. The French work is particularly valuable."

"Why is the French work valuable? And why do you say that the Cornell papers are not good? This is important, Lib. Please answer carefully."

"Yes, it is important. The Cornell papers rely on the use of Fourier harmonic analysis. That method has been discredited for this type problem. The French work—"

"Wait a minute," Keith interrupted. "Who says Fourier analysis has been discredited? That's been a fundamental analytical tool for decades. Who discredits it?"

"Mr. Robertson," replied Lib in a very condescending tone, "the inappropriateness of Fourier analysis for such work is well known."

Keith went to the next point. "And the French work? I've never heard of it before. Why do you believe it is worthy of our attention?" He found himself involuntarily adopting her debating tone.

"The French have become very innovative in this area. Their work has not been getting the attention it deserves. That situation is long overdue for correction. IP could gain praise by leading this revolutionary change." She sounded almost as if she were quoting someone. Keith had to think about this. There was no point in continuing to argue with Lib. He signed off with a brief, "Thanks, Lib. I'll get back to you."

Satisfied that he would learn no more on this round, Keith turned to leave. He saw Kim sitting alone, staring out the window. Poor guy, he thought, his dad's death hit him pretty hard. He walked over and laid his hand on Kim's shoulder.

"How're ya doin', guy?" he asked.

"Oh, I'm doing all right," said Kim unconvincingly.

"What's this I hear about you and the Community Rec Center?"

"Oh, it's no big deal. They let me set up a little pottery center in the basement there. Just a couple of wheels, an electric kiln, maybe a slab roller if anyone wants it. Plus the necessary tables, cabinets, file cabinets, sink. You know. Lotta people've never even seen stuff like that."

"Gee, that's great, Kim! Can anybody just go in and use it? Will they know what to do?"

"Yeah. I've started working with the middle school there. Those kids are about the right age. I'm giving a couple of the teachers some lessons. They've said they'll find the kids who are interested and keep 'em from wrecking the joint. And I'll drop by from time to time to see if I can help. Murph said it was okay," he added defensively.

"Gosh, that's wonderful! Your dad would have been real proud of you, fella!"

"Aw, it's no big deal. It's the least I can do."

SUNDAY, MAY 27: THE RUBINS'S HOME

A couple of days later, Keith got a call from Bob Rubin. "Hi, Keith! I've got someone here I want you both to meet. He's only here for two days, so I hope you can make it soon. How about tonight?"

They hurried over that evening and met Bruce Klingbeil. Thoughtful and kind are two words that nearly everybody applied to Bruce. Though he was soft-spoken, it quickly became clear that he was a man of strong convictions. He was a card-carrying, full-time, Christian Science healer. That is, he was formally certified by the Mother Church, and healing through prayer was his only source of income. But what interested Bob was that Bruce had embarked on a project to scientifically measure and explore how Christian Science healing worked. With scientific instruments, a computer, tables, charts, and mathematical formulae, he had already prepared a number of scientific papers on his research.

"Do you have a doctorate in an appropriate field of science?" asked Keith in his usual, direct way.

"No, I do not," replied Bruce with a slight smile. "I have had to learn what I needed to know through books and through consultation with scientists and statisticians."

"Well, doesn't that make it tough to get published and funded? I mean, no degree and no university or laboratory connections ..."

"It certainly does," said Bruce. "Maybe that is why I have gotten no outside funding and can hardly get other scientists to read my papers, let alone publish them. And I have been told that my writing style is alien to scientists. I grew up rather isolated, raised on the Victorian prose of Mary Baker Eddy and the measured cadences of the King James Bible. Scientists seem to find my writing dense and my thought processes alien."

Keith had noticed that although Bruce's accent was thoroughly American, he talked with the rhetorical precision one usually associates with foreigners. "Well, you must get a lot of support from the Church, don't you? I've read about how people have sued on behalf of children whose parents relied on Christian Science healing. The prosecutors claimed that praying was the same as doing nothing and that these were simple cases of child neglect or child abuse. And the Church didn't seem to put up much of an argument. If they had scientific data …"

Bruce's smile was now wide, but his eyes looked sad. "They have fought me every step of the way. They have publicly denounced what I am doing, they have told me to stop, and they are telling people to stay away from me. Other Christian groups have burned my books publicly, and the Church recently revoked my certification."

"That's like revoking a doctor's license," explained Bob. "He can no longer practice his profession. And I hear they are undertaking excommunication proceedings."

"I don't get it," said Keith, genuinely shocked. "How do they get heresy out of this? They object to putting science into Christian Science? Isn't that just what Mrs. Eddy taught?"

Bruce smiled, again sadly. "The objection is not theological; it is institutional. I believe the aspect that concerned them the most was the fact that if one could reliably measure the effectiveness of prayer, that ability could turn out to be a weapon of awesome power. It could give someone outside the Church hierarchy and beyond its control the ability to judge individuals in responsible positions in the church. These people could be declared unfit for their jobs—in a sense, their holiness could be judged, or at least one aspect of it. That is akin to the problem posed to the Catholic church by Martin Luther, who cried 'every man his own Pope.' He insisted that the church hierarchy was not necessary for an individual to reach an understanding of God and his duties to God. That position was deemed highly destructive to the church's ability to control its organization and determine its policies. It left teachings and practices open to challenge. Previously, change had only happened in controlled and well-defined ways that were dictated from above and within the organization."

Keith could only say, "Wow. I see what you mean. And even if you assured them you would never use what you learn as a weapon, they couldn't afford to risk it. I get it."

There was silence for a minute, and then Keith asked in a lighter tone, "What are you doing, anyway? Worshipping idols? Sacrificing virgins under the full moon? Give me some details. I really want to know."

"Maybe he will, if you give him a chance," mumbled Joan under her breath.

Keith ignored her, and Bruce replied, "We are actually measuring the rate of healing both under the influence of prayer and under neutral conditions—with no one praying—and demonstrating that there is a difference."

In such situations, Joan usually played the good wife, sitting patiently while her husband explored a subject of his choosing. But now she seemed fascinated by Bruce and what he was saying. Keith could see how it complemented and supported the psychic phenomena she had read about and her remarkable experience with Silva Mind Control. He could understand why she was listening so attentively.

"How do you measure healing?" asked Keith. "You're working with a hospital? What do you measure?"

"We do not work with human patients," said Bruce. "It would raise legal and ethical questions. And the human body is much too complicated to get simple measurements on how something heals. We started with rye grass seeds—thousands of them in little boxes—and measured the length of each blade as they sprouted. Very tedious. Then we tried mung beans and measured their weight gain as they grew. Then we tried yeast because it gives off carbon dioxide gas as it grows, and this can be measured easily and accurately."

"How do you get sick mung beans?" Joan asked.

"That is a critical point," responded Bruce, "because we found that healing prayer does not have much effect on a healthy organism. So we dried out the beans until they really needed water to regain their health, and then we measured weight gain."

"Very clever," murmured Joan.

"Cleverer than you might think," said Bruce. "It allowed us to measure the difference between faith healing and spiritual healing."

"Wait a minute," interjected Keith. "You'll have to explain that."

"I had intended to," continued Bruce. "It is quite important. We Christian Scientists have two types of prayer. The first is what we call directed prayer, and it may lead to faith healing. This is when someone prays fervently for a loved one to get well and has great faith that this will indeed happen. The faith may be based on God or just on the effectiveness of the medicine or the doctor. We found that this works, to some degree.

"The second type of prayer, which we call holy prayer or non-directed prayer, leads to spiritual healing. This is when we pray, 'Not my will, but Thy will be done.' That is very different from praying, in effect, 'Get well now! Get well!' Holy prayer proved to be much more effective."

"But how did you measure the difference?" persisted Keith.

"With the mung beans, we did some tests in which we over-soaked the beans. They were waterlogged. They had to dry out some to regain their health. So the 'directed pray-ers' were looking for and praying for weight increases, which is what they were used to associating with improved health. The 'holy pray-ers' just asked for the beans to achieve whatever was best for them. And you could really see the difference in the results."

Bob stepped in at this point. "Bruce, tell them about your work with random number generators. That will really hit Keith where he lives. Random number generators are just electronic devices," Bob explained to the Robertsons, "that produce a string of ones and zeros in a perfectly random order. Mechanical dice-rollers, really. You heard about that at Princeton."

"Why build computers to roll dice?" asked Joan.

"Because it's virtually impossible to produce dice that are really random," explained Bob. "All real dice are biased to some degree. If you scoop six dots out of one side and only one out of the other, the die will be lighter on the six side, and that side will tend to come up on top more often. Computers, of course, don't have that problem, and computers can do their flipping thousands of times per second."

Bruce resumed his explanation. "We hook these devices up to a little light that goes on when there are more ones than zeros and off when there are more zeros than ones. We demonstrate that the unattended machine consistently produces a balanced number of each, and we recheck those base conditions from time to time to be sure that the machine isn't drifting toward more ones or more zeros."

"But what's this got to do with healing?" asked Keith, anxious to get onto new ground.

"For you to understand that, I'll have to explain the Christian Science view of order and disorder and their relations to health and sickness," answered Bruce. "Do you want to get into that?"

"Sure, if it's relevant to understanding your work. Lay it on us."

Bruce almost visibly slipped into his teaching mode, a role he had found essential to doing both his research and his healing. Keith was impressed with his eloquence and with the depth and breadth of his understanding.

"The universe as pictured by Christian Scientists is filled with a pattern-generating, pattern-mending presence, a force or field that guides embryos toward birth and fulfillment and helps heal the sick and the wounded. This force affects inanimate objects as well as living things, forming the patterns in snowflakes and diamonds and maintaining the laws of probability. We equate this nurturing, supportive, healing force with goodness and mercy. We associate the forces that tend to distort and destroy patterns with evil. I maintain that the fact that this is an essentially religious view does not make it scientifically invalid. We go on to postulate that through prayer, we can tune into—or resonate with—that primal healing force and help focus it onto an entity that needs mending, like a sick person."

The fact that Bruce was tired and jetlagged was making his voice grow even softer than usual. Joan pulled her chair closer to him as he continued.

"I think that this worldview is consistent with Rupert Sheldrake's morphogenetic fields, Harold Burr's 'fields of life,' Bohm and Pribram's holographic universe, Jung's collective unconscious, Peter Russell's global brain, Persinger's and Tart's work on geomagnetic interference with ESP performance, and many other cosmic constructs that tie us all together and influence us in various ways. But we Spindrifters have examined this concept in different and more thorough ways. We've also followed its implications out into many new trails and compiled a significant amount of quantitative data on what we have found."

"What's this name, Spindrifters? Where did that come from?" asked Keith.

"Spindrift is a Scottish sailing term for the froth that a strong wind tears off the waves. It is the battered product of the interaction between two mostly separate worlds, the wind and the water. We felt that we were such products. We started using the term when some of the people who worked with us were punished severely by their own churches—both Catholic and Protestant—for publishing research results under their own names. Now everything we publish is authored by Spindrift. This prevents personal retribution …"

"… but raises a lot of eyebrows in the straight scientific community," finished Bob.

Bruce resumed his instruction. "If you believe that light is a wave, you can design experiments to prove it. Not until you decide that it may be more like a particle will you be able to devise experiments that demonstrate the totally different, particulate characteristics of light. So until you can see, feel, and 'believe' in the sort of universe we Spindrifters envision and try to understand how everything in such a universe would act and interact, you are talking at cross-purposes with people who almost never think about such things. That is why I am going into all this. Do you want me to go on?"

There were firm nods all around, so Bruce continued. "In addition to the cosmic pattern-making, pattern-mending force, Spindrifters attribute some powers to the human mind. Quantum mechanics requires that human consciousness interact with the physical world and teaches that purely passive observation is not possible. John Wheeler, the eminent physicist, once wrote, 'In ways we don't fully understand, observation seems to be a participatory process.' I previously mentioned the mind's ability to call on, focus, and direct the healing force to some degree. Spindrifters believe the mind also has some ability to extract information from the physical world—the ESP powers known to parapsychology. The Spindrift experiments seem to show that even an unconscious mind that has no apparent intent or focus can exhibit such powers, albeit to a lesser degree.

"In addition to these positive powers of the mind, Spindrift describes defense mechanisms, the functions of which are to hide the fearsome existence and extent of our psychic capabilities from us. If the mind guesses a few correct cards, a defense mechanism moves in to supply a few wrong guesses. If the mind creates order among a few digits as they emerge from the random event generator—or REG, as we call it—the defense mechanism disorders a few. This is the 'psi missing' phenomenon, also familiar to parapsychologists. But now the game gets interesting. If you run off a million digits from an REG designed to deliver about an equal number of zeroes and ones and then you count the total number of each, you will find they never deviate far from the norm. This is the standard approach of most REG studies in parapsychology, and the defense mechanism has an easy job here—it just has to keep the total number of 'misses' about equal to the number of 'hits.'

"The Spindrifters decided to go after the defense mechanism, to smoke it out into the open. Instead of just totaling up the zeroes and ones in a block of REG output, we began to look at the data points sequentially as they emerged. If the defense mechanism chose to follow up each bit of psi ordering with an equal and opposite burst of disordered points, such a pattern would be easy to detect. So we set up experimental protocols that gave the defense mechanism a minimum of options, and we were finally able to catch it *in flagrante delicto*. If you're going to understand how we did this, I have to back up and describe how we defined order and disorder in such a system."

"This is central," said Bob. "Listen carefully. You have to get this."

Keith had been to many seminars and lectures, but this was not like any of them. His recent psychic experiences and Bruce's low-key intensity gave his words authority and real-world relevance. He didn't want to miss a word. Looking over at Joan, he sensed that she felt the same way.

"We decided that the *natural* order for a system of ones and zeroes was a simple alternating series: 1, 0, 1, 0, 1, 0, and so on, and that the maximum disorder was 1, 1, 1, 1, etc. or 0, 0, 0, 0, etc. Now, one could view this the opposite way as well. You could say, I'll get these all in order by grouping all the ones together, then all the zeroes. But the idea of *naturalness* seems primary to us. We argue that if one saw a series of all zeroes or all ones coming from a random event generator, one would consider that very unnatural and would assume that something had distorted the natural pattern. By the same logic, you would reshuffle a deck of playing cards if you found too many cards of one type in a row. A healthy, human body with everything 'in good, working order' does not have all its similar parts grouped together. They are arranged in the pattern that best makes the total organism function well.

"This idea of a natural or 'naturally optimum' pattern comes from the Spindrift approach to healing. Our premise is that the omnipresent, ordering force works to maintain the natural pattern, which is a healthy organism that functions with full vigor and vitality, and that sickness is a departure from this naturally optimum pattern. We assume that this matter of orderliness applies to all parts of the system; in a person, the entire body has an optimum pattern in which it functions best, and so does each organ and each substructure within each organ. Similarly, in the string of numbers produced by an REG, one looks for patterns in each pair of digits in the sequence—are they orderly, like 0, 1 or 1, 0, or are they disorderly, like 1, 1 or 0, 0? But one can also look for order in groups of four, groups of eight, and groups of twelve. And one can look for pairs of pairs, etc."

At this point, Maggie walked in with tall glasses of iced tea, and the women exchanged a few words about the Rubins's latest travels. But Keith was anxious to get to the end of the explanation, despite the lateness of the hour. He finally said, "Bruce, explain a little more about the role of the defense mechanism. How do you know it's there, and what do you do about it?"

So Bruce picked up pretty much where he had left off. (*How does he do that?* marveled Keith.) "The purpose of looking for order in such small details of structures is to catch the defense mechanism at work. As I said earlier, the defense mechanism would not be very effective at hiding the ordering process if it merely let some order show itself and then compensated by producing exactly the same amount and same kind of disorder. Such a pattern is easily detectable. So the defensive effect is subtler. If we look at the 'normal' Gaussian curve predicted by statistics, we see a bell-shaped curve with the maximum number of ones or zeroes at the expected middle point and smaller numbers for the values on each side of the midpoint. The ordering force pushes the center of this curve up a little, and the defense mechanism raises the "tails" of the curve—that is, it produces more extreme deviations on either side of the mean that might be expected to counterbalance the increased number of points right on the expected target."

"Do you know that, or are you speculating?" asked Bob, who had been quiet up until then.

"Oh, we discovered that by looking at our data. The PEAR people found the same thing in their work at Princeton. The effect is small, but it is definitely there. And we did a lot of other experiments that involved interfacing with the computer. I cannot go into all of them now. But there were lots of them.

"I would summarize the significance of all these experiments as follows. We predicted that very strong, precisely defined deviations would appear in the data. We predicted that these deviations would possess the characteristics of patterns we'd found in random, binary sequences that we had generated in earlier tests. We predicted that these patterns would be interpretable in terms of the theoretical constructs that underlie our research effort in general and our work with random, binary sequences in particular. We predicted that the magnitudes of the predicted patterns would be less than the magnitudes of similar patterns produced by conscious thought. All these predictions were confirmed by the test results."

Bruce seemed to have come to a stopping point. Maggie said to him, "You must be tired. You're jetlagged, and you've been working hard. Do you want to turn in now?"

Bruce agreed without protest, said good night to everyone, and went quietly to his bedroom. Maggie went with him to ensure that sheets, towels, and the like were handy. Bob and Keith sat looking at each other silently while Joan took the glasses to the kitchen.

Finally, Keith said, "I'm sure getting a lot of input these days from people who are convinced that humans can distort computer outputs with their minds. And they seem to have lots of data to prove it. Bob, you've been around. You've been studying this stuff intently. And you're no flake. Tell me: is all this stuff for real?"

Bob replied, "You've heard the same stuff I have. You're a scientist. What do *you* think?"

Keith didn't bite. "Dammit, cut the crap! I'm not playing games. I've gotta know. You don't know how important this is to me. Could somebody be screwing up Libby mentally? Using some kind of voodoo curse? Could they?"

Bob didn't hesitate. "From what we've heard—and there's a lot more you haven't heard—it certainly seems possible." He smiled. "You know, Bruce's son John wrote a marvelous sci-fi story, book-length, about a bunch of bad guys breaking into government computers using only psychic intention—the same principle Bruce was talking about tonight."

Keith kept pressing. "If you were me, would you go to Murph McCarthy and suggest this? You've met Murph; can you picture me talking to him about this? Can you?"

Bob held his ground. "What are your other options? Have you got anything better? You tell me Lib is designed to be particularly sensitive to outside influences, to change its mode of operation, and to actually evolve toward what seems to be needed. It sounds to me like a perfect target for a psychic saboteur."

Keith sighed a deep, sorrowful sigh. "I was afraid you'd say that."

Joan didn't say anything. But her frown and her own deep sigh implied that she was even more concerned than Keith about where the pursuit of this scary subject was taking them.

TUESDAY, MAY 29: LIB'S "OFFICE"

The fact that there were troubles with Lib was now beyond dispute or denial, but the cause was as much a mystery as ever. In fact, the engineers at InfoPower even found it difficult to describe the nature of the problem as they tried to explain it to their management and to various outside consultants.

"We think we know what we have," said Kim to Keith and the others who had gathered to go over the situation one more time, "and then she gives us something that doesn't fit any previous pattern. Last night I got a whole series of 'Darwin Award' jokes, the kind of thing that keeps popping up in various chat rooms and listservs. Why would she give me that? I guess unpredictability is the only constant thread."

"Sounds to me like somebody's deliberately screwing around with the works," said Mike Kopliner, IP's "rent-a-cop" and all-around security agent. Mike's thick, Jersey accent initially gave the impression that he was a classic, thick-skulled flatfoot. But his rough exterior masked a highly trained professional. This caused many an adversary to underestimate him, always to their detriment, so he made no effort to change his ways.

"Know what I mean?" he continued. "Somebody's gettin' in there somehow and tweakin' a few valves ... or resistors, or whatever. We really gotta provide airtight, twenty-four-seven security on this thing."

"Aw, we got that already," replied Kim.

Mike didn't buy that. "Yeah? Can you guarantee that the machine is never unguarded? The guard never dozes off? Never even takes a leak? And can he see all sides of the machine, all doors and windows? Having only one guard on duty can never give ya complete protection. I keep tellin' that to Mr. McCarthy, but nothin' happens."

Ralph Belasco had another concern. Because he was the chief technical officer, everyone listened when he spoke up. "This machine is pretty sensitive to all kinds of electromagnetic fields. Could somebody shine a microwave generator or another kind of field generator at it, like the Russkies did to our embassy in Moscow years ago? We never really found out why they did that. Were they trying to tap our message signals? Or screw up our sensitive, electronic equipment? As far as I've heard, we still don't know. The embassy put up protective screens, but they still had an abnormally high number of employees develop cancer. Could that sort of thing be happening here? It should be easy to detect."

Fred Singer, one of Kim's new, hotshot electronics recruits, answered that. "Mr. Belasco, I had the same idea a few days ago, sir, and I ran an EM scan. As you said, that sort of thing is easy to detect. And I couldn't find any significant signal. I agree, you might really be able to screw things up that way, but we seem to be clean. I don't think there is any doubt about it, sir. You could have someone else check me on it."

But Belasco persisted. "Could someone work through the input voltage, impress some kind of signal or static without creating a detectable EM field?"

"Oh, no, sir," countered the kid. "All the input power goes through a standby power stabilizer. Its whole purpose is to smooth out any variations and feed a steady voltage to the computer no matter what. It's very effective; it rides through power outages, voltage spikes from lightning on the grid, all that stuff. I can't picture anybody feeding any signal through that."

"Could somebody tap in downstream, from the power stabilizer?" Ralph persisted.

Keith heard all this almost as though he were in another room; his mind was screaming at him to tell them about the psychics, the guys who could screw up computers with their minds alone. He wasn't going to blurt it all out here, not in front of this crowd, but he had to tell someone. He finally caught Kim's eye and signaled that he wanted to see him alone. After a few moments, Kim pulled away from the clump of people around him and edged over to Keith.

"You want to see me?" he asked.

"When you've got a minute," said Keith. "I want to go over something with you."

"I guess there isn't going to be a better time," said Kim. "Your pad or mine?"

"Let's go to my office," suggested Keith. "You've got too many people looking for you. Better yet, how about the little conference room?"

"Naw, there's a bunch of guys reviewing circuit diagrams in there. Let's go to yours."

They went down the hall and around the corner to Keith's office, out of sight of the lab and the crowd gathered there. Keith started tentatively, explaining that he wasn't trying to sell anything, he was just kicking around an idea. In fact, he wasn't sure himself whether it was even worth talking about. But Kim cut in bluntly.

"Look, Keith, we're old friends, and we've pushed some pretty crazy stuff together. Nothing you can say at this stage is going to change my opinion of you. We've tried all the reasonable ideas on this problem. Your outside computer gurus couldn't find anything, although they sure knew how to draw up an impressive invoice. We're desperate. Murph is about to make Lib into my funeral pyre. In this situation, no idea is too crazy to talk about. So don't beat around the bush. Lay it on me straight. What's your idea?"

Keith's mind spun its wheels for a moment, trying to decide where to begin. He had thought about what he was going to say, of course, but now it seemed that there ought to be a better way to break it to a down-to-earth engineer like Kim—and like Keith himself had been only a few months ago. But the pause grew embarrassing, so he just plunged in. He started with the punch line.

"I think it's possible that someone could be distorting Lib's operation merely by concentrating on making that happen. I've seen it done. I've seen some pretty scary stuff in the past few months. Just give me a chance to tell you what I've learned."

Kim was silent and nodded assent, showing no hostility, so Keith pressed on. He told Kim about PEAR and Helmut Schmidt and the Spindrifters and how they could alter a computer's output from any distance. He talked about the fact that over the past hundred years, thousands of scientific papers had been written about such mental effects and published in peer-reviewed journals. Sure, they weren't all flawless, but there were some very good ones, even though none of it ever got into the mainstream scientific literature. He talked a little about his experience with Silva and a few lab tests he'd run himself to show that he wasn't just buying into a lot of secondhand chatter. And finally, he ran out of steam.

Kim broke the silence. "So, what are you going to do next?" Keith knew the answer, but he dreaded it. "I guess I have to discuss this with Ralph or with Murph. But I have trouble picturing that going well. You're special, Kim. I can talk with you. I really appreciate that."

"You should probably talk to them both, preferably at the same time. Murph won't listen until he knows Ralph has bought in. And you don't want Ralph to try to explain this to Murph."

"Yeah, I suppose," said Keith dubiously.

"But you can't do it like you just did with me," said Kim. "Do you realize we've been here for more than an hour? They won't sit still for that. You're going to have to put all this down in a memo and get them to read it before you meet with them. And it will have to be short and crisp. Maybe with a longer, technical document attached. A tough job!"

"You've gotten to be quite the company politician," said Keith admiringly. "I'm the guy who's supposed to give you talks like that. Where'd you learn all that stuff?"

"You forget that I've been on the firing line for a while. You either learn or burn, you know that."

"Well, you're right, of course. I hate to do it, but there's no other way. Wish me luck."

WEDNESDAY, MAY 30:
IP'S EXECUTIVE CONFERENCE ROOM

Keith had worked on his report, rereading and reorganizing it until even he couldn't tell whether it made sense or not. He couldn't talk about it with anyone but Kim, and although Kim was sympathetic, Keith knew he was ultimately on his own on this one. Ralph Belasco wouldn't say much if Murph was in the room. Ralph was the idea man, and it was primarily his visions that the company carried out. So Ralph had the undying admiration and respect of every member of the IP team. But they all also knew that without Murph, the company never would have gotten off the ground. And it couldn't have kept going year after year, either. Ralph knew this too, so he was happy that Murph was around and was just the kind of guy he was.

But that didn't mean that Murph was easy to deal with. He was at his worst if he thought you were covering something up or holding things back from him. That wouldn't apply here. Murph wasn't much better if he saw a problem that you hadn't seen and if you didn't agree with his judgment about how serious that problem was. That didn't apply here either. He was at his best when you were reporting a problem and describing its implications and some possible solutions. It was incredible how gentle and understanding he could be then, even if the problem was your fault. He didn't want to give you any incentive to soften your description of the problem or hold back any details. (Your chewing-out would come later, after the fix was underway.) Maybe that was what would happen this time. But Keith knew that Murph's most predictable characteristic was his unpredictability. That's what kept everybody on their toes.

The time came when Keith knew he had to stop massaging the report and turn it in along with a request for a follow-up meeting. And when Murph's secretary called to say that he and Mr. Belasco would meet with Keith at 2:30, he knew that the Moment of Truth had arrived. He could almost hear the bullfight trumpets, and he wished he had a Suit of Lights and a sharp sword. When 2:28 came, he started down the long hall to the executive conference room.

Before he could sit down, Murph barked, "Let's not waste time. I've read all your stuff here. We don't have to repeat the arguments. Suppose I tell you I buy all this crap. What then? What do you do next?"

Keith now saw that Murph had already discussed this with Ralph and that Murph would be doing all the talking. Realizing that he would not have to deliver the half-hour summary of his report that he had been mulling over, Keith asked, "If we conclude that there is a possibility that a psychic—"

"—is putting a damn voodoo hex on our computer," Murph finished. "Yeah, that's what I'm saying. Then what? We hire an exorcist?"

"It seems to me," said Keith, "that we have to come up with a motive. Why would anyone do this?"

"I'll bite," said Murph. "Why?"

"Money seems the most likely incentive to me."

"Where would the money come from? I'm not sure where you're trying to go with this, Robertson," said Murph.

"I can see a couple of outfits that might pay good money to slow us down," said Keith. "Lib has caused quite a stir in the business. You've seen the articles. There've been some pretty flowery predictions about how Lib is going to put IP way out in front of the competition."

"Hell," said Murph. "We planted most of those stories."

"I know," said Keith. "But a lot of people are buying it, and there's some truth in the message."

"So you think—"

"What would it be worth to CyberTek or to P2P to be able to cripple Lib? Quite a bit, I would think."

"But can you just go out and hire a psychic like you hire a hit man to put a contract on somebody?" Murph was dubious. "Where do you find these characters? Are they in the yellow pages? Regular hit men aren't. And I thought psychics were supposed to be holy types, not hired guns."

"I don't know all the answers yet. I'm pretty sure I could find some psychics. But I think I'd start at the other end."

"What do you mean, the other end?" asked Murph.

"I'd start quietly investigating CyberTek. It's our closest rival. Let's see if they've got anything suspicious going on. Something like this would be hard to keep secret from everybody. Somebody will know something."

"Well, I'm not giving you time off to go play detective," said Murph. "If you really believe in this thing, you can follow up on it. But you're not to lower your chargeable time by more than twenty-five percent, and you've got to clean it up by, say, July 15. That's a whole month. And don't do anything that will get us sued. Now get back to work. We still have to meet payrolls around here."

THURSDAY, MAY 31:
IP'S EXECUTIVE CONFERENCE ROOM

Keith was really embarrassed. He could feel the flush in his cheeks and the trace of cold sweat that was emerging on his brow. He hadn't experienced this since high school, and he had long forgotten what it felt like. He was ashamed, too. But dammit, he hadn't done anything wrong. Well, he had to admit to himself that sneaking around and trying to find dirt on a competitor was not something to be proud of. It wasn't his style, and it wasn't IP's, either. But his secretary was saying, "It's Mr. Tarrantino, Principal Officer of CyberTek. He'd like to talk to you."

Maybe it's just a routine call, thought Keith. But he knew, somehow, that it wasn't.

"Hello, Joe. What can I do for you?" he asked.

"Keith, I heard you were interested in learning more about our outfit and how we work. Would you like to come over and let me give you a tour? There's not a lot to show, but I'd be glad to go over whatever you'd like to know." *Shit!* thought Keith. *How did he find out? It must be that damn psychic of his. That's it! The psychic!*

"Well, that's very nice, Joe. But I don't want to put you out or tie up your people. I know you're busy."

Keith felt he had to say something else. *Why am I making this visit? I have to explain this somehow.* "Joe, uh, there've been some indications of industrial sabotage—or rather, I guess you'd say attempted spying. The boss insists I try to track it down. That's all. Sorta silly, but you have to humor the bosses. You know ..." *That sounded kinda dumb. Wish I hadn't said it.*

"Glad to do it. We work the same vineyard; we ought to get to know each other better. Can you do it today, maybe at lunchtime? I'm leaving town tomorrow, and I don't know when the next chance will be."

"Uh, sure, Joe," said Keith. "Noon?"

"Fine. I'll have some sandwiches and stuff. We'll use the low-overhead cookies, and it will hardly cost us any chargeable time. Gotta eat sometime, right?"

Keith looked at his watch. *This doesn't give me much time to plan my tactics. Maybe that's why Joe made his preemptive strike. He gets to define the battlefield and the timing. And he's on his own turf. The guy's not dumb.*

He decided to drive over to CyberTek. He hated driving in the city, but the subway didn't go over to Old Town Alexandria, and cabs were really expensive. It was a nice day, the drive along the Potomac River was serene, and it gave him a chance to collect his thoughts. He wasn't sure how he could uncover any nefarious activities; he'd just have to wing it and hope for a break. *In any event, I'll get a chance to find out how this outfit works,* he thought. *They're supposed to be a very professional gang with high ethical standards. Well, we'll see.*

He spotted the CTek logo on a handsome, red brick, Colonial-style building in Alexandria's Old Town. Some of the streets that continued a few blocks down to the river still had cobblestones dating back to George Washington's day and possibly almost a century earlier. On the riverfront itself, the new docks and boat clubs reflected little of the days when Alexandria was one of America's foremost seaports. The ugly torpedo factory, built for World War I, had been spruced up and converted into hundreds of art studios where potters, weavers, painters, and silversmiths did their work; they had become major community assets. Old Town looked like a nice place to work, and Keith couldn't help wistfully contrasting it with IP's hectic and expensive location across the river on K Street Northwest in downtown Washington DC. Joe had saved a parking place for him in the building's lower level, and from there he took the elevator up to the company's reception area.

Joe Tarrantino came out to greet him. He was tall and thin, with swarthy complexion and a closely shaven heavy beard. A few years earlier, he had trained for the Iron Man Triathalon, a killer competition including swimming, bicycling, and running. He had burned up more than six thousand calories per day; he had gotten up to work out at 4:30 each morning and gone running again every night. He had no dreams of entering the Olympics; he just did it for personal discipline. Despite eating like a hog, he had begun to look like a skeleton in a skin suit, so he gave it up. But he still retained some of that over-trained look.

During Joe's years as an engineering officer on a nuclear attack submarine, his hands-on approach to engineering had given him a deep scar along the first finger of his right hand. Despite his master's degree in nuclear engineering and other specialized training, he never lost his practical sense of machinery, plumbing, and electrical systems. He was an engineer's engineer.

Joe walked Keith to the executive conference room, where a secretary took their orders for a Spartan meal of tuna sandwiches and Evian waters. Tarrantino took Keith on tour of the offices, where they talked with a few of the employees along the way, and then they returned to eat lunch. Keith was impressed by a number of things. He learned that the firm's own design and drafting people had laid out the workspaces, eschewing showiness for simple functionality. It was distinctly attractive. *I wish we'd done as well,* he mused. *Our offices are okay, but they look so ordinary.*

The CyberTek people were busy. There was no loitering, horseplay, or window-gazing, and yet there were no signs of managerial pressure. The employees seemed self-driven and reasonably happy about it. In addition, they had been lavishly supplied with top-grade equipment: computers, copiers, and a well-equipped mail room and report-assembly facility. And there was almost no display of the pecking order. The offices of the principal officers were no larger than those of the senior engineers. There were no fancy, outer offices for big shots; the company's money had clearly been spent to enhance the employees' ability to do a good job.

While they were in the conference room, Joe brought in one of the engineers to explain a particular project from time to time, but mostly it was just the two of them. Keith gingerly probed around, asking more and more intrusive questions, testing the waters. But Joe was relaxed throughout the meeting and answered his questions without hesitation or equivocation. *Wow,* thought Keith, *we wouldn't answer questions like that from a competitor.*

"We never hire a person just for a particular contract," explained Joe. "When we hire someone, it means we have just made the company one person bigger. Consequently, we've never had to lay anyone off for lack of work. We've had lean times like everyone else, and we've had a couple of years without bonuses. One year, we took a vote, and everybody agreed to take a temporary pay cut rather than lay people off. The other side of that coin is that there is not a single employee we'd be willing to lose. Now, I don't mean we've never lost or fired anybody, but our attrition rate—the number of people who leave each year for reasons not including retirement—is only about four percent, and that's been steady for a couple of decades.

"We also promote people from within to pretty responsible jobs. Because there is no job here that is unimportant. For instance, if we get a new engineer just out of college and put him with a secretary who's worked here for years, that's a winning combination. The secretary knows all sorts of stuff, like who is supposed to get copies of what, and everybody knows they're important to the company."

He grinned. "And we have the best damn office parties in the world, bar none. We try to do everything first-class. The gal on the copy machine, the folks in drafting—we don't want any detail to be less than it could be."

Keith cut in. "So how do you make money that way?"

Joe hit that one head-on. "That's very seldom a problem. When we have trouble keeping the cost of a job down, it's almost never because some fellow is trying to do it too well. Our trouble always turns out to be that an inexperienced engineer isn't getting enough senior guidance and is burning up hours without producing much. We find that our customers want excellence, and they're willing to pay for it. I've had top management people call and say, 'We'd like you to review a project for us. My people keep telling me it's just fine, but I've gotta know. And I know you folks will tell me what's right, not what you think I want to hear.' Those are the kinds of people that come to us."

Keith didn't want to let that go. "How do your people respond to that? When they're nearing the end of the job's budget, don't they want to start cutting corners? What do you tell them?"

"They all know that we consider it the manager's job to ensure that standards don't slip. That's more important to the company's health and survival than whether we make or lose a few bucks on a particular job."

"You obviously have top people. Don't you have pay better than most in order to get them and keep them? And then how do you compete and still make a profit?"

"There several parts to that issue. First, we do lose many competitions because our hourly rates are high. Some jobs go to companies that have lower-cost labor. We try to tell those buyers it's going to cost them more in the end. And it does. But some buyers' first priority is to convince their bosses that they got the lowest costs. I can't do anything about that except remind them what happened when they come around for the next bid.

"Yes, we pay well, but we seldom pay absolute top dollar to bring in a person. We don't want anyone who is coming just for the money. So we have to convince people that they'd be happier here for less money than they might be elsewhere for more. And we remind them that the one-time prize for coming in the door is less important than how things go year after year. We also have another objective: we really pay attention to taking care of our lowest-paid people. Have you heard of Kevin Phillips, who writes about business ethics? He says that a company should try to pay its lowest-paid employee one-seventh as much as its top-paid executive. Few companies do that, but they should set that as a goal. Remember when Ben and Jerry's made a big splash about doing that and then had to back off sheepishly when their top people demanded more? We've actually managed to maintain that ratio through the years."

"That's pretty noble, Joe. But is it really economically practical?"

"We're still in business. And our executives eat pretty well. We think one reason it works is that all our employees are loyal, and the fact that they have lots of experience enables them to minimize bloopers that would otherwise cost us a bundle."

Keith wanted to go back to an earlier point. "You said you promote from within. Give me some examples. In the flat organization you've described, what promotion opportunities are there?"

"We're a small outfit," said Joe. "We've got just over a hundred engineers and other professionals plus about thirty support staff. Over the years, we've had four secretaries come to us and say, 'I can be more than a secretary. I can do chargeable work.' And in each case, they've figured out how to do that with our help and encouragement. That's just one example."

"Doesn't that lead to a lot of in-house squabbling? Jealousy in the ranks?" asked Keith.

"No, quite the opposite. Everybody figures that about three-quarters of the people here are smarter than they are, and they welcome any help they can get. We did have one interesting challenge, though, but it turned out to be no problem."

"What's that?" asked Keith.

"Many years ago, all of a sudden, our campus recruiters reported that there were a few women engineers and black engineers showing up for interviews. We hadn't seen that before. As I said, we're a tight little family, and we wondered how they might fit in. The women were members of women's engineering organizations, and the black ones were in the black engineers' society. We worried, would they be political? If they didn't work out, could we get rid of them? Our selection process is very personal and subjective. We've turned down some candidates who were number one in their classes because they just didn't seem like our type. This kind of personnel action could, of course, be interpreted as illegal. Would women or blacks complicate this situation, sue us, and bring the whole place down in flames?"

"What's the answer?" asked Keith. "What happened?"

"Nothing, of course," laughed Joe. "They all worked out just great. In fact, the first female engineer and the first black one, both of whom we hired years ago, are still here and doing fine. But we had to educate the male chauvinist pigs. I had to tell them, 'You can't refer to them as "lady engineers" unless you're willing to call yourselves gentlemen engineers. If they can't hold their own simply as engineers, they don't belong here.' But, as you see, it all worked out."

Keith couldn't believe how willing Joe was to share all his secrets. "We don't really have any secrets," Joe insisted. "We get customers because of our own people's talents and our own approach to things. You can't steal that; nobody can. I'm sure it's the same with you people. Yeah, we compete with each other, but there are no secrets I could tell you that would give you an unfair advantage over me. I just don't worry about that."

Keith had one more question. "You've indicated that you have some very different types of people who have worked out well—some who are very innovative but not very thorough or very hardworking but not as productive. What criteria do you use to decide whether to keep a person?"

Joe's answer was simple. "We have a simple process that sheds light on that problem: people vote with their feet. When people are assigned tasks, they immediately set out to get others to commit the hours they need for the task. An employee wants to get the most for his money, and he probably knows his fellow workers better than I do. There are some people here who are always in demand. Others have to struggle to keep busy. That process makes it clear who's best and who's not as clearly worth the cost of his salary. Do you know a better way?" Keith did not.

After a very long "lunch hour," Keith was convinced that he had learned all he could about CTek. In his clandestine investigations the previous week, he had arranged for an intermediary to offer the company a lucrative but somewhat shady deal, and CTek had turned it down without discussion. He knew what he'd have to say to Murph. Driving home, he rehearsed it. *This outfit is clean. I can't believe they're involved in anything shady. They're tough competition for us because they're good. We should be so good! I think the glowing stories we've heard about CTek are true. They are proving every day that high-class technical work and high ethical standards can be profitable. The employees really like working there, and there are clients who go back for more. I guess we'd better start checking out P2P. But this time I'm going to go about it a little differently.*

But there was still the nagging question: *how did Joe know I wanted to check up on him?*

SATURDAY, JUNE 2: THE RUBINS'S HOME LIBRARY

Bob Rubin's library seemed even more cluttered than usual. In addition to the journals, newsletters, and books, there were now several stacks of notes and letters. *How does the guy ever find time to look at all that stuff, let alone digest it?* wondered Keith.

"Sorry to bother you on the weekend, Bob, but can we mix a little business with pleasure?" He had been hesitant about calling on a holiday, knowing that the Rubins would probably have other plans. But Bob had been so eager to get involved that he urged Keith to come right over. Bob's experience with Silva and his growing interest in the work of Spindrift had increased his long-standing fascination with mysteries, and he was as anxious as Keith to explore, and hopefully to solve, the mystery of the erratic librarian.

Bob nodded agreeably as he set down a couple of cold beers, and Keith went right to the point. "How're you doing on the witch hunt? Have you found any promising psychics for me?"

"I've covered a lot of ground since you first asked about that," began Bob. "And that wasn't very long ago, you know."

"Yeah, I'm sorry to be pushy. But I really feel the heat on my back. Lib's going from bad to worse, and everybody knows I'm supposed to come up with some magical solution, but I don't get to talk about it. I can't hold Murph off much longer. Do you have anything yet?"

"I've got quite a bit, as a matter of fact." He handed Keith a pad of paper. "You might want to write some of this down. They're quite a mixed bag, but that's what you need. I haven't asked for any commitments yet, but if you want action, we'd better be prepared to start pinning people down."

Keith asked the next question rather gingerly. "If these are all ... well, let's say holy sorts of people ... or maybe spiritual is a better word ... what I'm getting at is, do they take money? Can you discuss contracts and stuff like that with them, or would they be offended? I've never dealt with these kinds of people."

Bob grinned. "Sure you have. You said both Jahn and his lab director at Princeton were able to do this stuff. Did they seem unduly holy? These people have to eat, just like the rest of us. Bruce Klingbeil and other Christian Science healers get paid. Healing is often their only source of income."

"Okay, forget I asked. Bruce would be great, incidentally. Could we get him?"

Bob looked at him solemnly for a moment, then said, "I didn't get a chance to tell you yet. Bruce and his son John, who were the brains and the sweat and the major reporters on the Spindrift program, finally completed a big, fat, technical report on all their work. They self-published it and made it available to the world. Then Bruce said, 'We've put it all down. We've answered all the questions and criticisms we can. We've condensed and rewritten for clarity. There is really nothing more we can do on our own. There is no point in running more and more of these same tests. If anything comes of this, it will have to be through the replication and extension and revisions of others. We can do no more." Bob paused. "And then they bought a couple of shotguns, walked off into the Oregon woods, and killed themselves."

Keith just sat there, staring at Bob and replaying those last words over and over in his mind. He couldn't believe that Bob had been so cruelly blunt. But then he realized there was no way to break such news gently. "My God! Do you mean it? That kind, gentle man! He just wanted to help humanity, and everybody fought him on it! How awful! What a loss!"

Neither of them said anything for quite a while. Then Keith pulled himself together; he had to go on with the evening. He'd have to deal with Bruce's death later. Now, thinking about it just numbed him.

"Who've you got so far, and how did you find them? And how do we separate the real ones from the charlatans?"

Bob responded in kind. "I started by going to Anne Winfield. I think I introduced you to her some time ago. She's a full-time, professional psychic. She has a little office in the area, and people flock to see her—they have for years. She does counseling, which is really a form of healing, and laying-on of hands. She does séances and has been a featured speaker at national Spiritual Science conferences. She's a marvelous metal bender and works well with scientists. She and the late, great Olga Worrall were mutual admirers. I think she would work with us, and she helped me get in touch with the others I'm about to name. Have you got that? Anne Winfield. Do you need any more on her right now? I've got a write-up on each of them; I'll give them to you when we're through talking."

Keith nodded for Bob to continue, and he did. "Then there's Beverly Cardoso. She has a black Umbanda Spiritista great aunt who raised her for a few years when she was growing up in Brazil. Now she's a highly credentialed, widely published scientist; she's well respected in the parapsychological research community, but she's known to have personal powers as well. She teaches at one of the U.C. campuses in southern California—I forget which one—and does psi research there with money she brings in herself, kind of like what Bob Jahn does. She's probably available for a week or two, but she'd wish to work anonymously to protect her academic standing. Okay?"

Keith nodded, scribbling furiously, and Bob picked up a third folder. "Here's a good one: Dean Baumgartner. He works at a small, privately funded science frontier lab in Texas. He's frequently published in the psi journals. In fact, he's been president of the Parapsychological Association and is working on a book about the whole field. A really solid scientist, but also a person who gets positive results on the strength of his own personal psychic abilities. You know, this field has a number of really good scientists who seldom get interesting, positive results when they use themselves as subjects. They're good researchers, but they don't seem to have much psychic power of their own. This fellow does."

Picking up the fourth folder, Bob continued. "Now for something entirely different: Larissa Gardoff. She published a psi journal in Moscow all by herself during the darkest days of the Cold War. It was in English, and it was read all over the world by the small number of people who follow this field seriously. She did a special issue on fire-walking, gathering material from all over that had never been published before. Spectacular photos. She came to America once to take a crash course in Chinese; she just wanted to learn to read it well enough to translate abstracts of Chinese psi research papers. Spent some time in Israel. I don't know how she could do all that when the lid was on so tightly in Russia. I think she's in America now, and she might be available. Ready for one more?"

Keith nodded again, still scribbling. "Boris Drake, a mysterious and mystical freelance psychic. Sometimes strikes me as a little scary—he somehow always makes me think of Dracula. He's done some very dramatic stuff with out-of-body travel, where he floats up and reads numbers on a little shelf near the ceiling. His astral body—or whatever it is—trips electronic alarms when he does that, even while his physical body is lying quietly in bed in another room. He's also worked with scientists."

He paused. "That's everyone I've got right now who seems usable. There was an Eskimo, the grandson of a Siberian shaman, who did some pretty exciting stuff in my basement lab, activating electronic strain gages from a distance. But he announced one day that he was going 'back north.' And then he was gone, along with some of my books and papers that I had given him to read. And there are others who are not available or not appropriate for various reasons. But five psychics are enough to run a Delphic Circle."

"What's a Delphic Circle?" asked Keith dutifully.

"That's when you gather a group of psychics—usually seven, but five will do—and have them independently answer a question," explained Bob. "The answer has to be something you can quantify. For example, you might be looking for treasure and have a map. Each psychic independently draws a line around the area on the map where they believe the treasure is hidden. They each have separate maps, so they can't see what the others did. Sometimes there's a great deal of overlap, and then you can be hopeful that you're really getting valid information. Other times, the circles or ovals they draw are nowhere near each other, so you conclude that for whatever reason, they're not homing in on the target."

Keith was trying to figure how that would work in his case, but he jumped to the final, critical question. "Do these characters really produce results?" he asked. "I mean, we're not trying to tell fortunes for little, old ladies. We've got a real-world problem, and something real is going to have to change it. Bob, have these people ever gotten any real results, the kind I need?"

"I'll tell you the same thing your stockbroker tells you, Keith: past performance is no guarantee of future results. But there is some history to make us feel like it's worth trying."

"What kind of history? Give me some examples."

"In our society, we decide whether results are real by seeing if anyone will pay for them. Anne worked for the CEO of a major oil company for twelve years. She flew with him in a small plane over potential oil well sites. She'd say, "Here," he'd mark it on a map, and they'd drill there. He thought her record was good enough to keep paying her, and paying her well. She's found lost persons and lost objects and healed some people that the doctors couldn't help, including at least one U.S. congressman. This is her full-time profession and her only reliable source of income. I can document similar stories for each of these people. They're pretty unusual people, but they make a living through competition like all the rest of us. Some of their stories are in the folders I gave you. I can get more, if you need them."

Keith shook his head. He was tired and overloaded with information, and he had to get on with it.

"Do you want me to see how soon we can get them all together?" asked Bob. "If one or two of them have to join us via E-mail or conference call, I guess we could figure out how to do that, too."

"Yeah, go for it," said Keith wearily. He couldn't picture himself explaining all this to Murph. *If it works, we'll just go with the answers. If not, we'll just write it off and move on. The less said, the better*, he figured.

MONDAY, JUNE 4: LA MADELEINE RESTAURANT

Keith looked around the restaurant with its faux French country inn decor. An eight-foot waterwheel was slowly rotating a large millstone through the action of hand-hewn, wooden gear-teeth meshing with a bird-cage-like, wooden master gear on the shaft of the wheel. The twelve-inch, square, solid, wooden shaft on the millstone matched the exposed, dark beams in the ceiling. The water from the mill splashed into a pool with tall, ornamental grasses and other appropriate plants growing in it. An old washboard hung on one wall, and some carpentry tools and old-fashioned kitchen equipment hung in other spots. A large, wooden cabinet with glass doors showed bedsheets and towels, neatly folded for some mythical, future use. The bookshelves in a side room were crammed with old books of various types. And in a large, brick fireplace, a gas-fired flame licked around fake logs despite the July heat that challenged the air conditioning. The bakery, whose large ovens produced a continuous stream of tasty breads, rolls, and croissants, filled the air with its wonderful aromas.

The restaurant had been there only a few years, and despite all the fakery, it had managed to become a neighborhood meeting place and look the part. An ever-changing array of local paintings, photos, and other pleasing evidence of the artistic community's vitality hung on the walls. French classes were held there, and a tour of France was being discussed. You could often overhear spirited conversations in French going on at a couple of the tables. Keith smiled as he remembered that Joan had first seen these same sights in a similar building with the same name in the Quartier Francaise in New Orleans when she was down there for a pottery conference. *We sure don't have this sort of thing in Bethesda*, she had thought, only to discover when she returned that just that sort of thing had recently opened up a few miles from her home. Only then did she realize that it was a national chain.

Keith had picked this place for lunch because it was on Rockville Pike, which was convenient to a number of "Beltway Bandit" technical contractors on Interstate-270. These included Power to the People, abbreviated to P2P, IP's other significant competitor. Keith had visited P2P only once. The offices were a little gaudy for his taste. The big shots had big offices and private outer offices with leather couches and fancy curtains. One even had a large American flag on an eagle-crested flagpole, just like an admiral's office. But hidden in back was a large, warehouse-like room with scores of Dilbert-reminiscent cubicles for the low-paid employees. The types of work the company accepted to keep these Dilberts occupied was dull and repetitive, but it kept P2P's average salary cost competitively low.

Keith was meeting an engineering colleague named Manny Manelli, whom he ran into from time to time because they attended many of the same meetings, trade shows, and conferences. Keith had gotten to know several of his business colleagues that way, and he had gotten quite friendly with some of them. Manny, who was easy to talk with and was a great source of information, was a good example. Manny had worked for P2P for several years, but he had been laid off the previous year and was now working just down the street for a similar but smaller outfit. Manny was a talkative guy, and Keith hoped to get a feel for whether P2P might be the kind of firm that was willing to hire a hit-man to clandestinely foul up a competitor's computer.

His thoughts were interrupted when Manny walked in, only a few minutes late. The big smile that lit his vaguely Mediterranean face always gave Keith a lift. Wherever Manny went, he got the same reaction: *good old Manny!*

Keith knew Manny liked pasta, so he had already ordered a bottle of Chianti. He felt sure that Manny would drink at least half of it, and if things ran their course, Manny would soon be telling locker room stories about life at P2P. After the obligatory verbal horseplay and after Manny had drunk a couple of glasses of the wine, Keith said, "Y'know, I don't think we've had a good talk since you left P2P. How did that go? Was it a good place to work?"

Manny gave an uninformative answer, so Keith needled him gently with a couple of leading questions. Once Manny got into his storytelling mode, Keith could just sit back and listen. You could say what you wanted about Manny, but when he got going, he could sure tell one good story after another.

"Is Johnny what's-his-name—Johnny Buck—is he still as slippery as he used to be?" asked Keith. "They used to say Johnny could enter a revolving door behind you and come out in front of you. Or is he losing it in his old age? We all begin to lose our edge at some point. What's he up to these days?"

Manny took the bait. "Hell, no! He's not losing it. Sharp as ever."

Johnny was high up in the technical sales department and was one of the company's important role models. If P2P were to make any effort to improve its image, they'd have to tone down Johnny. Manny started telling an anecdote about another of Johnny's outrageous pranks, a recent one. Keith wasn't interested in the details; he was beginning to feel like he already had his answer. But Manny told it anyway.

"Now, this wasn't illegal or anything, y'understand. Legal, yes. Legit, no!" and he roared his Manny laugh. "We bought some equipment for a plant—as a third party supplier, y'know. Manny could get us a cut and still get the buyer a better price. Well, this equipment was a very special pump. Had to pump very hot water at high pressure. Specially designed for this plant. Well, they had tested the pump at full temp and pressure, and it looked okay. But when the plant guys installed it on a cold, winter day, they threw the switch and nothin' happened. Nothin'! Cold water is heavier than real hot water, and it's more viscous, too. And maybe the plant voltage was a little low that day or something, but anyway, the stupid pump wouldn't start. It just wouldn't start.

"So all hell breaks loose, and Johnny has to go over to the meeting and explain it all, since he was the guy who convinced 'em to buy it through these guys. Well, they're all shouting at him and yellin' for an answer, and Johnny is just sitting there looking through the pump manual. So the president of the company—the pump buyer, that is—grabs him by the shoulder and says, 'What about it, Johnny? You got a good answer?' And what do you think he says? Guess what the silly son of a bitch says?"

Keith shrugged his shoulders, and Manny continued. "He starts talking in a low, relaxed tone, as if nothing had happened. 'I been reading the specs,' he says to the gang, and now they've all quieted down to hear him. 'You know, there's nothin' in here that says the pump has to start cold.' And the other guys tear the book out of his hands and start looking through it, while Johnny quietly clips his fingernails. Then he suggests, in that same mild tone, 'If you'd like to add that additional requirement, I could probably get you a good price on it.'" Manny threw back his head for another guffaw that attracted the attention of the people at several adjacent tables.

"I don't know how it all came out, but how about that? They never said the pump had to start up cold."

He took another cut at the Chianti bottle, then said, "Well, one trick Johnny learned and passed on was one you've been bit on, Keith: bid low, then make it up on the change orders. I've seen them underbid you and a lot of other guys with prices everybody knew they couldn't meet. Then when the job finally winds up, the total cost is way above the other bids. But they get paid—or at least they get most of it—because they keep makin' parts of it change orders. Everybody knows from the start that that's what they're gonna do. But the lawyers and the auditors make companies give jobs to the lowest bidder, and then they bitch about the change orders a year or two later. By that time, they don't even have the same purchasing people—or the same lawyers, for that matter."

After a few more stories in the same vein, Keith had had enough and decided to go in for the kill. "How come you left, Manny? I never heard."

Manny didn't hesitate on that one. "You know the old song, Keith. 'First they hired me, then they fired me, then, by golly, I left!'" He roared at his own good humor, but Keith pursued it. "You're good, Manny. You've been around a while, you know the ropes. I'm surprised they let you go."

Manny got more serious now. "Aw, Keith, you know how these birds work. They hear about a big job that would require them to hire forty more people for a year. If they're lucky, they can get it extended a couple of times. So they go out and hire forty warm bodies. They try to get good ones, but the order is, 'Bring in forty warm bodies.' Then, if they don't get the job, or if they don't get an extension a year later, they gotta lay off forty people. I know you guys just wouldn't bid on a job like that. You'd tell 'em you don't have the manpower. But P2P never turns down a job. 'We'll handle it somehow' is their philosophy. They promise to put a lot of senior people on each job, but after they get the contracts, you'll never see those fellas on the sites. They send in the kids, the untrained recruits. In fact, they have no real, dedicated training program that's carried out on overtime—it's all on-the-job training, paid for by the client. You saw the news report that they decided to shut down their office in Paris and make other reductions? Eight hundred and fifty people laid off. Eight hundred and fifty! That's the way they operate. Then their big marketing department revs up more advertising, they take out more hospitality suites and hand out more free booze at trade shows, and they keep recruiting as if they'd never laid anybody off."

Keith nodded understandingly. IP and CyberTek never did things like that. People kept telling them that you had to in order to survive, but they were surviving just fine. P2P operated on the more conventional pattern.

Manny was warmed up now and deep in his storytelling mode. Keith refilled his wine glass, and Manny told story after story. There was nothing really outrageous, but a couple of the capers he talked about were a bit shady, and many more were less than entirely professional. Even accounting for any exaggerating that Manny may have been doing, it was not a pretty picture. In addition, Keith couldn't help recalling the big Navy contract out of which P2P had beaten IP before Keith had joined them. Everyone agreed that IP should have had it, and there was talk that money had been passed under the table. But Murph had be unable to verify that anything illegal had happened, so he'd told the troops to forget it and move on. Keith had accepted that story at the time, but now he was not so sure. And he certainly had no problem picturing P2P deciding to jinx a competitor's critical machine. Now he had to figure out how to catch them at it.

TUESDAY, JUNE 5: IP CEO'S OFFICE

As Keith waited outside Murph McCarthy's office for Ralph Belasco to join him, he realized that he had seen more of these two men in the last few weeks than he had in all the months preceding. He didn't mind talking with Ralph; Ralph was more like a colleague than a boss. He admired Ralph tremendously, but they talked engineer-to-engineer, and Keith never got that conference-with-the-boss feeling. But Ralph's low-key modesty was misleading. Just when you felt you were chatting casually with a professional equal, Ralph would come up with a critical insight or piece of information, and you were reminded again why he was chief technical officer and you weren't.

Murph was different. Oh boy, was he different! Whatever the topic of conversation, you always knew you were in the presence of The Boss. Because Keith had had so many meetings with Murph lately, the tight feeling in his stomach wasn't as severe as it used to get. But it was lurking there, and a knot could appear in an instant; the feeling stood quivering and at the ready, so to speak.

Ralph arrived right on time. They walked up to the secretary's desk, and she buzzed Murph's phone and said, "They're both here, Mr. McCarthy."

Murph barked, "Show 'em in," and they entered quickly and took the two chairs in front of his desk. The secretary quietly closed the door behind them.

"So, what did you learn?" asked Murph.

Keith knew enough to have a well-prepared oral report ready. He also knew that his chances of getting to deliver it were slim. But there was no other alternative. You prepared your spiel and started to deliver it, and then Murph threw the whole thing off track by asking something totally unexpected. People said that Murph was unpredictable, but that was one thing about him that you could predict with confidence.

The other thing Keith had learned was that with Murph, you had to give the punch line in the opening sentence. This approach always made engineers and scientists nervous; it seemed backwards. They liked to start where they knew they'd find agreement: *you'll agree that we're having trouble getting that new software to respond fast enough, right?* Then they'd go to the next point of agreement, and finally, after the problem had been defined, spelled out, and agreed upon, they'd present the conclusion they were trying to sell: *so it seems to me that what we have to do is ...* But everyone knew not to try that approach on Murph. He'd shout, "Where are you trying to go with this? What's your point? I'm not agreeing to anything until you tell me what you're trying to sell me!"

So Keith started his story, feeling like the straight man on Groucho Marx's show. "Sir, I believe that P2P is capable of trying to jinx a competitor's information system."

"What do you base that on?" asked Murph.

"Well, they seem to measure everything by the bottom line," said Keith. "Profitability is their major measure of merit. They—"

Murph exploded. It was not the rage that preceded a major dressing down but rather the kind that foreshadowed a sermon. "Dammit, Robertson, don't you go equating a keen eye for profitability with immorality or unethical behavior. A company that loses concern for profitability, even for a few months, withers up and dies. If you chip-heads didn't have somebody like me hovering over you every second and continually watching the implications for profitability in your every move, we'd have gone out of business years ago."

His tone changed. With a sardonic grin, Murph said with mock humility, "I apologize, Robertson. You're not a computer jock, are you? I called you a chip-head. I should have used the more respectful term for mechanical engineer: flange-head."

And he returned to his sermon. "You techies just don't get it. I fully understand that your ideas and technical savvy are essential to getting ahead in this business. Good God, if I didn't understand that, I wouldn't put up with you characters for another day. But that's not enough! It's really not enough. Look, we humans have to breathe to stay alive, right? Otherwise we die. But no amount of breathing can do away with our need for food. If we don't eat, we also die. I've never bought the business school mantra that the purpose of business is to make money. That's not only immoral; it's also just not true. It's like saying that the purpose of living is to breathe. This company exists because the state gave us a license, and the license says that they give us certain legal privileges and protections because they expect us to contribute to the good of society. And I know that's part of why you guys are here. Don't you think I'm here for that reason too?

"You know what I do at the office picnic each year? I look around and see a couple hundred people, plus a lot of kids. Each of those people has urgent financial commitments—mortgage payments, car payments, installment payments for getting his kid's teeth straightened—all those legal obligations before they can even start paying for food and clothing. I look at these people, and they don't look like they're worried sick about all those obligations. And why not? Because they get the same paycheck every Friday without fail. They count on it. And that doesn't happen automatically. If we let them down, they would all be in a panic. As each job ends, we have to have another to fill in behind it. Not more than we can handle, but enough to keep everybody fully occupied on chargeable time. That's what it takes to deliver those paychecks. And if we ever failed those people—our people—then all you guys'd take a different attitude toward those of us who worship the bottom line. I think it's immoral to take a cavalier attitude about the bottom line; we have a sacred duty to all those people. They're counting on us."

He paused. Keith knew better than to say anything. Murph continued, "I know P2P's CFO. He's not an evil guy. I think he's driven by the same demon I am—he wants to help a lot of nice, smart guys make wonderful stuff that will lead to a better world. And all that sentimental shit. So don't tell me that the fact that an outfit worries about profitability proves that they're immoral."

Wow! thought Keith. *That's sure not where I expected this conversation to go.* "Then you don't think they would do something like this?"

"I didn't say that," barked Murph. "Anybody might do it under the right circumstances. I also know their chairman. He's a real shark."

Keith didn't know where to go from there. Murph said, "We're not getting anywhere on this thing. If these psychics are worth anything, they ought to be able to tell us if somebody's fouling up the psychic airwaves. But let's not waste much more time on this. Get back to me next week."

THE DELPHIC CIRCLE

SATURDAY, JUNE 9: SPIRITUAL SCIENCE CENTER

Keith didn't get over to 16th Street very often. It wasn't far from his home, but the things that happened there had always made it seem like a different world from the one he'd inhabited. Now, however, as he headed for his meeting with Bob Rubin's psychics, he found himself reacting differently to the neighborhood's contrasts and contradictions, which lived boisterously shoulder to shoulder.

The meeting was at the National Spiritual Science Center of Washington DC. It had been a Washington fixture for decades, albeit one known only to a devoted few. The Center taught courses and arranged workshops in various spiritual, religious, philosophical, and metaphysical subjects through the Center's Spiritual Science Metaphysical School. It was located in a wonderful Victorian mansion among the many that lined Washington's Gold Coast on Upper 16th Street, Northwest.

The Center also had meeting rooms for visiting speakers and other activities consistent with its agenda, and Bob Rubin had been there a number of times. It was located conveniently close to the Rubins's and Robertsons's homes, so Bob had rented a conference room there for the day.

Keith was fascinated by the drive down 16th Street from East-West Highway in Maryland down into the District of Columbia. The side streets passed in rapid succession, all named for decorative plants: Primrose, Myrtle, Iris, Hemlock, Holly, Geranium ... Then the names assumed an orderly, alphabetical procession that started downtown. First, there were the streets named for the letters of the alphabet, followed by one-syllable words in alphabetical order, then two-syllable words, and then three-syllable names: Whittier, Van Buren, Underwood, Tuckerman ...

The neat, rectangular grid of Washington's named and numbered streets was designed by the talented city planner Pierre L'Enfant and reflected the militant rationalism of eighteenth-century France. The design created many beautiful city squares and circles, but it also enabled these focal points to be quickly outfitted with cannons to control unruly mobs. L'Enfant planned things this way in case the recent French Revolution inspired similar uprisings in the fragile, new American capital.

Ornate brick and stone mansions of many designs nestled comfortably into L'Enfant's theoretical abstraction. In obeisance to the changing times, many had elaborate wrought-ironwork covering the doors and windows. In some houses, the ironwork was painted white or even robin's egg blue. These buildings now housed a bewildering variety of cultural and spiritual institutions: the Bahai Faith; the Chanceries of the Republic of the Congo and the Republic of Liberia; Chua Giac Hoang, or the Buddhist Congregational Church of America, and the Buddhist Vihara; The Owl School (N-8), The British School of Washington and the Lincoln Multicultural Middle School; St. Jude's Serbian Orthodox Church; St. Stephen's Episcopal; St. George's Antiochian Greek Orthodox; Grace Lutheran; the Talmud-Torah Synagogue and School; and the Shrine of the Sacred Heart. Keith also saw the Washington Ethical Society, the National Dental Association, and a brightly colored, seven-foot-high sculpture of an African mask.

Finally, he reached the Center, pulled onto a side street, found a parking place, and walked up the steps and into the old mansion. Looking around the beautiful, old meeting room with its high ceiling, ornate, curtained windows, and heavy, wooden table, he thought, *If they had designed this room for a movie about psychics, they couldn't have built a better stage set.* Bob was already there with his psychics, or "sensitives," as some of them preferred to be called. And a variegated assemblage they were. Bob jumped to his feet, offered Keith a chair, and said, "We're just about ready for you. We've been going over some preliminaries and answering questions. And I guess we're about ready to start. Aren't we?" he asked the group, and they nodded assent.

"You've met Anne," he said, gesturing toward Anne Winfield. "As I told you, she is a professional, full-time psychic. She's worked for some heads of major corporations on special projects, and she does counseling and healings, locates lost objects, and has spent considerable time working with researchers pro-bono and trying to understand how these special powers of consciousness work. She is also a person of some repute in the Spiritualist Church and has performed some amazing séances, providing very personal advice from departed friends and relatives that has often proved to be of great value."

Anne was also a very attractive woman. She had light-brown hair of medium length and conservative makeup, was nicely dressed, and wore a modest amount of good jewelry. She would have fit in and been accepted in any company. Keith could picture her in her small, all-pink office that Bob had described to him. She was soft-spoken but obviously strong. Keith figured that her serene demeanor probably made her look younger than she was. Bob had said that she had a grown daughter, so he knew she was not as young as he would have guessed.

Next around the table was Beverly Cardoso, a psi researcher at one of the University of California campuses. She had a dark, Latin beauty that was muted by her severely tailored suit and the fact that her long, black hair was pulled back in a tight bun. *She'd look great in a long, red dress with her hair down,* thought Keith. He remembered Bob talking about her black, Brazilian, spiritista aunt and wondered what other exotic ancestors went into creating that kind of face. She said that she had deliberately decided to be up-front with her academic colleagues about the consciousness research she did and then to offer few targets for criticism by keeping her experimental techniques impeccable and her dress and manners professional. Her doctorate was in statistical design of experiments, and her array of papers in the field had helped her *modis operandi* work, at least so far.

Dean Baumgartner was another cat altogether. Big and rumpled, he had left college before graduation to become one of the "young Turks" who had surrounded J. B. Rhine at Duke University. Starting in the 1930s, Rhine took psi research out of the séance parlor and brought the ghosts into the laboratory. He was determined to apply the new science of experimental psychology, which was bolstered by emerging techniques in statistics, to what he called parapsychology. This included studying what he renamed extrasensory perception, or ESP—the practice of gathering information mentally—and psychokinesis, or PK—mentally influencing the physical world. Baumgartner was one of his best disciples. He became president of the Parapsychological Association in the late 1950s and worked primarily in the area of mental interaction with computers, where Jahn and Schmidt had done so well. Keith was pleased to have him on the team.

Larrisa Gardoff was not at all what Keith had expected. Somehow, he'd thought that she'd look more Russian. But as he thought about it, he realized he didn't really know what that meant, especially considering the wide variety of ethnic groups that lived in that vast country. She looked like any young-to-middle-aged American: pleasant, a little tired, a little heavier than ideal, and casually dressed. She was not at all striking for a person who had such broad, intellectual accomplishments. Her English was excellent. She was both a scientist and a "sensitive," an experimenter and an editor, widely read but down to earth. Her background and skills were very different from that of the others. As Bob said, that was an asset.

Boris (he pronounced it bah-REECE) Drake was the biggest mystery. He was of Eastern European heritage—Bob never did find out which country. Keith liked to think he was from Transylvania, although he had also sort of been picturing him like Rasputin ever since he had heard Bob's brief description of him. He had some unpronounceable last name, but in America he went by "Dr. Drake," which made Americans think of Dracula. He had a resonant, commanding voice and deep-set, penetrating eyes set in a dark, crease-lined face. Keith could easily see how he might have the hypnotic powers attributed to him. He had been both experimenter and subject, specializing in trance states and out-of-body research, and he told some pretty spooky stories about what had happened under those conditions. It was rumored that he had done work for the CIA, but of course he wouldn't confirm or deny those rumors, as they say. He just smiled enigmatically when asked. Keith was not quite sure how he would fit into this team, but he was glad Boris was on his side. They sure wouldn't want him as an adversary. He reminded Keith of stories he had heard about Wolf Messing, the Polish-born psychic who reportedly managed to walk past all of Stalin's guards "invisibly" to catch Stalin alone and had performed many other extraordinary feats for him. Bob had said that psychics were just like everyone else, but this gang was not like anyone Keith knew.

When the introductions were complete, Bob began to outline why they were there and what they had to do in the immediate future. He seemed to be addressing these remarks to Keith, but Keith figured he did that so as not to appear condescending; he was saying things that at least some of them would probably take for granted. Bob wanted to be sure that everyone started out with the same basic information about where they were, where they were trying to go, and how they were going to try to get there. Bob never took such things for granted, and Keith was glad of that.

"Keith," he said, "what we're going to do here is called a Delphic Session, named after the Delphic oracle in pre-Christian Greece. We are asking for information and advice from beyond the physical world, just as the ancient Greeks and Romans did, but that's about the only resemblance to their procedure. We don't have any Greek goddesses or Vestal Virgins here. But the idea is that when any one person tries to get information from the beyond, it doesn't come through in a neatly organized, staff-memo format. It's usually in images, phrases, hunches, and metaphors, mixed with snatches of things from the psychic's daily life. There is no sure way to know which of the pieces are crucial and valid and which are irrelevant or unintelligible. So we ask several sensitives the same question, and they compare notes. If the psychics get a lot of agreeing pieces, we take those areas of agreement and try to build a 'consensus oracle' that presumably gives a better answer than any one of them could have given alone." He paused. "But there's no guarantee that it will work at all, of course."

"The trick—as it is in all experiments—will be to ask the right questions. You can't get good answers if you don't have good questions. Another important aspect, which I think we've already handled, is to get the right psychics. Psychics are not all skilled in all aspects of the art. We've found, for instance, that many people who seem to have no other psychic skills at all do very well at remote viewing. They can perceive through ESP what a particular, secretly chosen location looks like although they have never seen or heard of it. And conversely, there are people who are particularly skilled at healing. Others are good at séances and others at prophesy, but these people may not have well developed skills in other areas. I took all of this into account before selecting the people we have here in this room."

He paused, looked around, and gathered his thoughts. He took a long drink of water, grinned, turned to Keith, and said, "Did you know that many people believe that it's very important to drink plenty of water before attempting any psychic task? There are also indications that fluorescent lighting tends to interfere. And geomagnetic disturbances caused by solar flares and other extraterrestrial activity can interfere as well. You'll note that this room has no fluorescent lighting, and we've checked that the geomagnetic level here is not bad today. So we've avoided all the pitfalls we know about. We have worked out several different approaches, and we will try as many as we seem to need."

He grinned again. "May The Force be with us!"

MONDAY, JUNE 11:
THE COSMOS CLUB

Keith was really crushed. All that psychic talent had homed in on his little problem, and he had nothing to show for it. *Nada.* They had tried several different kinds of exercises, but they never got an adequate degree of agreement, nothing they could turn into a solution. They had sent the psychics home. And Murph had called a meeting of everyone involved in the project for the next day.

Keith couldn't understand it. He had personally witnessed several demonstrations of psychic power that were clearly not magic tricks. But when the chips were down, the psychics had failed him. His frantic efforts to make sense out of what had happened just spun in circles. In a desperate effort to try anything that might help, Keith had shut himself in his bedroom and had tried to "go to his level" a la Silva. Alone, he felt self-conscious and tense. When he got to his meditation room, the opening doors revealed his counselor, but it was not the wise, old, Asian man with whom he'd grown comfortable at Silva. It was Lib! Startled, he ejected from his trance state and looked around the room, trying to reorient himself. *What did that mean?* He got no answers and was left feeling vaguely dissatisfied.

He had to talk with someone, but he couldn't talk about it with anyone at the office. Not yet. Nor was it the sort of thing he could talk with Joan about. He had to talk with Bob Rubin.

He had called Bob and found out that he would be doing literature research at the Cosmos Club library all day. Bob suggested that Keith join him there for lunch. That sounded like a great idea. It would be quiet, and they would not be disturbed. Besides, he had always wanted to see the inside of that august building. Taxis would normally drop you off at the imposing entrance on Embassy Row, across from the Ritz-Carlton and the colonnaded Society of the Cincinnati. But taxis were expensive, so Bob had given him driving instructions.

He had driven into the Club's obscure parking entrance off 21st Street and entered through the back door of the elegant, French Renaissance mansion. The walls of the corridor were covered with bold, colorful paintings by a Club member. When he turned into the main hallway, he saw photographs of all the members who were Nobel laureates and Pulitzer Prize winners, followed by a display of members who were featured on postage stamps from all over the world. Bob explained that the building had once been the home of Mrs. Mary Scott Townsend, who was a model "hostess with the mostest" starting at the beginning of the twentieth century. Her lavish parties had included the most prominent political, social, and intellectual figures, and thus they became important mechanisms for settling many issues of the day. Keith could easily believe that the Club still served that function.

They went into the gracious dining room, and along with their menus, they were given hot popovers, straight from the oven. Skipping the niceties, Keith proceeded to tell Bob everything he had been thinking, ending with, "So we got absolutely nothing out of this. I feel conned! Is this whole psychic thing a fraud? Did we pay a bunch of con men to play tricks on us?"

"You know the answer to that, Keith. If you ask some mainstream, scientific authorities, they'll tell you there's nothing to it. And the more emotional they are about it, the surer you can be that they've never looked at the data. I don't have any problem with a scientist—or anyone else—deciding that psychic phenomena are not worth looking into. But then they don't have the right to make judgments on the subject. Unfortunately, that's exactly what too many of them do. They can't find any fault with the experiments, so they laugh them off by saying that ESP stands for 'error some place'."

Keith didn't buy that as an answer. "Are you telling me that the wild stuff I saw never happened? Or that it was some sort of parlor trick?"

"No, of course not. No one can deny someone else's experience. You've also seen some of the scientific reports. Some of them are published in peer-reviewed, mainstream journals. When J. B. Rhine first published his mind-reading experiments at Duke in 1934, the top statistical authorities said publicly that even if anyone wanted to quarrel with his results, they couldn't fault the statistics on which the conclusions were based."

"Well, I don't care about the mind-reading stuff. But what about this business of influencing the physical world by just thinking about it? That's what I'm concerned with."

"Rhine did that, too," replied Bob patiently. "He didn't have computers, so he used dice. Some professional gamblers claimed they could control the dice, so he tested them in the lab. It turned out that some of them could. And, as you saw, Jahn and Dunne did the same thing with computers fifty years later."

"Yeah, I know. But that was a very tiny effect."

"Actually, he tells me that the interest he gets from mainstream physicists is mostly in those carefully controlled computer runs that are reproducible, run after run, and have been replicated by other scientists in other labs. They point out that the first experimental proof of Einstein's theory of relativity was the predicted gravitational bending of the light of Mercury's orbit around the sun. It was almost too small to measure even with the best instruments. But it was reproducible. Anybody could check it, and many did. Now it's beyond question."

"Okay, but where does that leave me? Why did our psychics fail? Are they just not very good psychics?"

"No, they're among the very best. You've seen and read about some of the things they've done."

"Then what happened? What does all this prove about Lib?"

Bob sat up a little straighter and said slowly, "Let's narrow the focus. What specifically were you trying to get out of the psychics? What did you want them to do? Think for a minute before you answer."

Keith flushed a bit as he realized he'd been pretty vague about that. But he answered, "I had reason to believe that someone had a motive to interfere with Lib's operations. And after seeing some of the effects that people could cause on computers, I thought that our adversaries might have had both the incentive and the means. I wanted to see if the psychics could confirm that. Or disprove it," he added quickly.

"And how do scientists design experiments to prove or disprove things? What's the general rule?" asked Bob.

"You mean the null hypothesis?"

"Right! How does that work?"

"Well, in this case, if you think there's been a psychic attack, then you try to disprove it by controlling all the other variables that might have caused it, and if it still shows up, then you've proved it. That is, until a smarter guy comes along and proves that the problems are caused by something else."

"Fair enough. And did you do that?"

"Well, not really. In fact, Murph implies there's another possibility, and he's going to talk about it with us tomorrow."

"Then have you proved *anything* with the psychics?"

"Well, yeah. Yeah, I think so. I dug pretty deep into their claims, and I'm convinced there is something there. They're not phonies. If they can detect psychic stuff going on, and they didn't find any, maybe it's because there isn't any. Maybe Lib's problems aren't psychic."

"How do you feel about that possibility?"

"I hadn't thought about it before, but I think it makes sense. At least until we learn more."

"I agree. You now have a basis for discounting your fear of psychic tricks played by your competitors. That's probably a healthy change, and it's good from a business standpoint as well as for your own mental health. It sounds to me like your psychics didn't fail; they gave you what you needed, although it wasn't what you expected. You were convinced that CTek had a psychic spy, when it was probably just the old business rumor grapevine."

Keith had to agree. "Yeah, and some good did come out of all this. Joan actually came down to the office and spent quite a bit of time with Lib, researching Bud's illness. She didn't actually find a solution, but she learned a lot about his condition, and she gained a lot of respect for Lib—and some sympathy for my problems with her. And not only with Lib, I guess; I think she also got some insight into her own problems with me. She seems to be getting a little easier to deal with, and she's not so quick to hit the bottle when she gets frustrated. I've got to be thankful for that."

"Absolutely! I've been worried about you two. Maybe Lib can begin to be a resource rather than a rival."

"Yeah. Joan also got so much information on Anne Winfield's successful healings that she decided to pay her a visit with Bud."

"What came of that? You never told me about that."

"Well, it just happened last week. He had one session with her, and he's feeling much better. They're going back again this week. She thinks she may be able to do him some real good."

"That's great, Keith! This is the first thing that has ever really done Bud any good, right?"

"Yeah, that's right. We feel pretty good about it."

But he didn't feel any better about tomorrow's meeting with Murph.

TUESDAY, JUNE 12:
IP'S EXECUTIVE CONFERENCE ROOM

Keith had lost the ball, and Murph was going to call the next shot. Keith hated that, but he had to concede that he didn't know what the next move should be. This whole mess had settled on him like a poisonous cloud. He couldn't even think straight. His mind just went around in circles, and he kept coming back to thoughts he had already discarded. *Damn!*

Murph walked in with Ralph in tow and sat at the head of the table, where his seat had been saved. He had another man with him as well, whom he now proceeded to introduce without any preamble or explanation.

"This is Don Waterman. They tell me he's a complexity specialist and an independent, expert consultant on artificial intelligence systems. He damn well better be. One thing we seem to have here is complexity. Dr. Waterman has published widely in this field and either knows what he's talking about or has hoodwinked a lot of smart guys. Ralph has explained our problem to him, and he thinks he can help. I've told him that if we don't get this thing straightened out fast, we'll be scrapping a pretty expensive computer system. I've handed you copies of his qualifications so that you'll be properly respectful in dealing with him. Of course, if he screws up, he's just another bum as far as we're concerned. Don, give 'em your pitch."

Waterman was handsome but not pretty. He was a big man, but he was trim and well dressed. He looked more like a business executive than a scientist. Keith judged from his silver hair and his firm, clear complexion that he was sixty, maybe sixty-five, and that he probably worked out regularly. His voice was confident, and he spoke smoothly in long, clear sentences with no *ums* or broken thoughts. Maybe he did know something. Keith sure hoped so.

Waterman started right in. Taking his cue from Murph's no-frills opener, he hit the ground running. "Complexity is not the same as complication. Building a 747 airplane is complicated. Very complicated. There are literally millions of parts, millions of steps, millions of procedures to perform, and hundreds of thousands of people involved. But if a wrong part or a bad weld is installed, the plane will make no attempt to adapt to this change. It just won't work right. So being complicated doesn't make something complex.

"'Complexity' denotes a system in which many semi-autonomous parts are trying to work with one another. They're continually talking back and forth. 'I want more heat,' says the thermostat. 'You're getting all I can give,' says the furnace. 'I'll keep pouring it out until you've had enough.' 'I'll tell you when I've had enough,' says the thermostat. So that's the first requirement of a complex system: various parts, each with its own needs and purposes, interacting with the other parts.

"The second requirement of a complex system is that it be adaptive—that it change itself in response to imposed changes and that it keeps trying to optimize its functions and its well-being as it gets different outside inputs. A colony of bacteria responds to an antibiotic by developing new strains that are resistant to the antibiotic. The stock market responds to a sudden demand by raising the price of that item. And the price will keep rising until the demand, which is also adaptive, responds by diminishing until the two come into balance again at a new price level."

Keith marveled that Waterman didn't make any of the distracting physical movements that ruin many other speakers' messages. Many times, Keith had found himself mesmerized by a speaker's meaningless gestures or nervous mannerisms to the point where he'd completely lost the thread of the talk. Waterman had no such flaws. *I guess that comes from his giving lots of talks like this,* thought Keith. But he had to admit that the man held his interest.

"A third characteristic of complex systems," continued Waterman, "is that they are capable of spontaneous self-organization—spontaneous in the sense that there is no direct order coming down from on high and telling them to reorganize. It's just how the system adapts. And here's where the surprises come in. Very simple, little algorithms—sets of rules—can create incredibly beautiful, sophisticated, and totally unexpected structures. You cannot predict how this is going to work out any more than you can predict a cathedral—or a dungeon—from the pile of stones used to build it. And you can't repeat it.

"I see some eyes glazing over, so let me give you an example. Let's build a tree out of a very simple algorithm. Let's take a computer program for drawing pictures and tell it, 'Go straight for one inch, then branch into two. Repeat indefinitely.' That's an algorithm—just a simple set of rules."

He went over to the white board, picked up a dark purple marker, and illustrated the process as he talked. He drew a short, straight, vertical line with two stubby lines branching off the top of it. "That's the basic procedure," he said. Then, from each of the stubs, he drew a line with two branches at the end. "That's the first repeat. And to make it more tree-like, I'll add the command, 'Make each branch 10 percent thinner than the one before it.'" He kept the process going until he had drawn a very intricate and bushy tree that was completely symmetrical. It looked as if it had been drawn by a very meticulous but rather simple-minded child. "This is pretty sloppy, so let me show you how a computer does it." [*See figure, next page.*]

"You can get all this from that simple, four-step rule," he said. "And we could go on from there. Let's say that one-third of the time there should be two branches (as we have now), half the time there should be three branches, and one-sixth of the time—that does make one hundred percent, doesn't it?—there should be four branches. And we can ask it to curve occasionally. These simple rules, followed automatically and repeatedly, produce amazingly complicated and lifelike pictures of plant forms. [*Next figure.*] Since the lengths and angles of each branch vary randomly, we cannot replicate any design. Each example is unique. And we cannot even reproduce any particular example again.

"If I had shown you this latter figure first and asked you to write a set of equations or a computer program to create this figure, you might well have believed that this was a task of monumental difficulty, at or near the limit of human imagination. Yet, we've seen that such figures can be drawn with a few very simple instructions.

"Let me emphasize," warned Waterman, "that I cannot reproduce any of these figures. No one can. They evolve without any externally applied control. Attempts to control them from the outside lead to the kind of messes we're seen people make of the environment, the economy, or the human body, when they try to modify its characteristics. Richard Dawkins tried to create pictures of ferns this way, and he ended up with a wild variety of insect-like shapes. They were beautiful and interesting but not at all what he expected or intended. That is why I'm telling you all this.

A "tree drawing" created by a computer program with just four instructions: "Draw a one-inch vertical line. Make two branches at 60 degrees. Repeat seven times, Make each branch 10 percent thinner than the previous set." It looks somewhat tree-like, but its perfect symmetry and repeated hexagonal figures do not make it look like a natural, living object.

(Computer drawing by Nevin Hoke)

"We're all used to working with systems that are orderly, that behave as expected. But we know that some things don't work like that—ocean waves, for example. No matter how hard we've tried, we've never been able to find a way to predict the height of a wave at a given point in space and time. Then, recently, some theorists came along with a new way of looking at such systems; they called it chaos theory and said it was a way to analyze unpredictable things. Complexity is the science of working with situations that surf along the boundary between order and chaos. And anybody who has tried surfing along the leading edge of an ocean wave knows that it's mighty tricky. But the rewards of learning how to do it are great.

The previous computer program was modified to make the lengths of lines and angles of branches vary within a range rather than be fixed numbers. There are no other changes. But now the four-step program produces a unique design that is asymmetrical and cannot be reproduced. This looks more like a natural tree.

(Computer drawing by Nevin Hoke)

"When the people at MIT were trying to build the first super-robot, they made it more and more complicated, trying to make it as smart as a human—or at least get closer to that goal. It weighed a ton and a half and was hooked to a wall-full of computers. But it took a long time for it to even figure out how to make its way across an uneven courtyard, and even then it was clumsy. But the little ants were scurrying casually around 'without brains in their heads,' so to speak. And the scientists decided that maybe the way to achieve really complex movements was not by making a more sophisticated central brain. Instead, they decided to make a number of simpler controllers and software that controlled each leg or other body part. There would be no central control system involved in those simple, 'instinctive' or 'reflexive' actions. There was some biological research that said that maybe this was the way animals worked, including us."

He paused, looked at his notes, and then looked up at the ceiling for a minute. He seemed completely unembarrassed by the silence. Then he looked down and continued. "There's another aspect of this that we'd better get into: emotion. When people interact, they always take emotion into account—or at least they should. If an argument with a colleague is turning into a shouting match, one of the parties usually says, 'Hey, let's break this off until tomorrow. I've got something to finish up tonight, and I'd better get on it.' Our machines don't work this way, and we don't expect them to. So occasionally, some chap shoots holes in his computer.

"We say, 'Friends don't let friends drive drunk.' But should your car keep you from driving while drunk? The auto companies looked into things like making you punch in some tricky code before the engine would start—something you supposedly couldn't do drunk. Nader got them to make cars (for a while) that wouldn't start until your seatbelt was buckled. But that's pitting you against your own car, and that's not the right way to go. It made my wife furious. When her car wouldn't start, she was not grateful for its assistance. She'd shout, 'Curse you, Ralph Nader!'

"The MIT Media Lab people are fixing up a Volvo to sense your stress level, perhaps through your breathing rate or pulse or the pattern of your voice, and say 'You're getting pretty tense, Dave. You've had a tough day. Why don't you stop and get a coffee and a doughnut.' Scary, eh? Sounds a bit like HAL in the movie *2001*. That's obviously not what you've got with Lib, but I'm just trying to tell you that we'd all better get used to computers that 'feel our pain' and think they know better than we do. I gave Murph a couple of books for your library—your old-fashioned library with real shelves and books in it. One's called *When Things Start to Think,* by Neil Gershenfeld, and the other's called *The Age of Spiritual Machines: When Computers Exceed Human Intelligence,* by Ray Kurzweil. You ought to look at them. They describe some of the sorts of problems we're running into here."

Waterman paused again, riffled through his notes, looked at the ceiling again, and pulled out one specific page. Then, in a more businesslike tone, he resumed. "I could go on for hours about this stuff, but let me leave you with one thought about dealing with an intelligence that seems out of control. When you have a complex, evolving system, you cannot control it from the outside. The legendary Chinese philosopher Lao Tzu understood this. Six hundred years before Christ, he wrote the following in the *Tao Te Ching:*

> Intelligent control appears as uncontrol or freedom. And for that reason, it is genuinely intelligent control. Unintelligent control appears as external domination. And for that reason it is really unintelligent control.
> Intelligent control exerts influence without appearing to do so.
> Unintelligent control tries to influence by making a show of force.

"I leave you with that thought, which is just as valid today as it was then. And now I am open to taking your questions."

This sudden ending took the group by surprise. People turned to their neighbors and mumbled perplexed questions. Murph interrupted the palaver by banging his fist down on the table and shouting, "If you have any intelligent questions, address them to Dr. Waterman. Otherwise, pipe down!"

A young engineer with long, stringy hair, glasses, and a prominent, throbbing Adam's apple tentatively raised his hand. Waterman pointed to him and nodded. The young man cleared his throat and asked, "I've read Dawkins—you know, *The Blind Watchmaker*—and he claims, well anyway, it seems to me he sorta argues—that plants and animals and even people may have been built up that way. You know, no God, no designer, just dumb algorithms. Is that right? Is that really the way it is?"

Waterman smiled benevolently. "That's a pretty wild and scary thought, isn't it? Yes, that's precisely what I'm talking about. Dawkins is a very smart man, and his whole book makes a very convincing case for what you just said. I encourage all of you to read it. But as for whether that's really the way it is, no mortal knows—at least not yet. Will we know some day? That's one of those questions that makes the future worth waiting for."

Murph cut in impatiently. "Anybody who wants to talk theology or metaphysics can pay Waterman's outrageous hourly rate out of his own pocket. Right now, let's stick to talking about Lib."

That cut the next half-dozen questions off at the ankles, which is just what Murph had intended. There was an embarrassed silence as each member of the audience choked off the universal questions that were on the tip of his tongue and tried to wrestle his mind down to earth. Murph grinned sympathetically, "All right, I know you all want to throw around the big questions and implications of this thing, and I'll give you some time later. But first we've got to discuss what we're here for. Try to focus on that."

Keith felt he had to kick off the discussion. "Dr. Waterman, I guess I don't know how to go about applying what you said to the problem we're having with Lib. If you're saying we have to reverse-engineer it, I wouldn't know how to start doing that. Could you give us some guidance, please?"

Waterman smiled again. Keith couldn't help thinking, *Sure, he can smile. He's going to walk out of here in a little while and collect his fee, and we'll still have to fix the problem.* Waterman understood his unspoken rebuke. It was the classic response to an outside expert. As a consultant, he faced it on every job. He knew that now was the time to respond to it.

"Look, I know it's easy to talk in generalities and sound like an expert. But that doesn't solve problems. And if I can't help solve problems, people won't hire me." Help was the key word here. "So I have as much incentive as you do to see this problem solved. And I don't have any illusions about solving it all by myself by waving a magic wand. That would make me look smart and make you look stupid, and nobody can attract customers that way. So even if I could, I wouldn't."

He paused and looked over the group. "I'm no smarter than you folks are—well, maybe a bit," he said with a big grin. "I bring certain information, experience, skills, and techniques to the table, but you people have accumulated months of design and operating experience with Lib, and that's the bulk of what we're going to need. If we lick this thing—or I should say, *when* we lick it—we'll all look good. Nobody's going to look bad. And that's what we all want."

He kept right on talking without a pause, but his tone had changed; it was no longer personal and confiding, and he now sounded brisk and businesslike. "To get back to this man's question ... Keith, is it?" Keith was in the front row, and Waterman could read his name badge. "Keith, you're on the right track. When a machine repeatedly malfunctions, you don't just beat on it. You have to find out what makes it do what it does. Is a control valve stuck? Has some tiny sub-routine program been corrupted or distorted? Once you find the malfunctioning part, you fix it or replace it, and *voila!* Everything works just like it should."

He paused, looked intently at Keith, and started speaking more slowing and deliberately. "That's what you do with an *ordinary* machine. A machine is supposed work in a perfectly predictable way all the time. That's how you can tell when something is wrong: it behaves differently. But Lib is not like that. You've put a lot of time and money into making Lib better than an ordinary machine. Lib learns and adapts and changes. No matter what you do to fix her, she will never act like she did before. She is more like a person than a machine. That's why you all instinctively found yourself unable to keep calling her "it." I called our dog "it" for a few days, but I quickly realized that he was definitely a "he," not an "it." I even did that to our baby for the first few days."

Waterman smiled appreciatively at the chuckles he received, but he returned quickly to business when he glimpsed Murph squirming restlessly in his seat. "After a person suffers a life-changing event—a traumatic war experience, a brutal divorce, a first love—he or she behaves differently," Waterman continued. "No one is surprised by this. When a person behaves strangely, we send him to a shrink, and the shrink doesn't berate him for behaving differently and tell him to resume the kind of behavior him showed before. No; the shrink tries to find out why that person's present behavior seems reasonable to him. She assumes that the person is still rational and that his current behavior makes sense for reasons neither the shrink nor the person's friends understand yet. Once they understand—once they can see the world the way the patient sees it—then they can argue about whether the behavior is really reasonable. And they can carry on this argument on the same ground as the patient."

Murph jumped in at this point. "Okay," he snapped. "so what do we do about Lib?"

"'What would you do with a friend who acted like this?' countered Waterman. "Someone you liked and respected?"

"I guess you'd have to send 'em to a shrink," conceded Murph, who would never go to a shrink himself but who knew what the expected answer was. "Can you do that to a machine? I mean, would any self-respecting shrink work on a machine? We don't have a big enough couch!"

"I'll concede that most practicing psychologists would not be willing to undertake such a project," admitted Waterman.

"Well," said Keith hesitantly, "you may think this is a dumb idea, but ..."

"Out with it," snapped Murph, who was always quick to "help things along" when someone was trying to figure out how to say something.

"The people who know Lib best—I mean, in terms of personality, or whatever you want to call it—are our psychics. They'd probably be our best bet for something like this."

"Oh, great," sighed Murph. "I thought we were through with those characters." He rubbed his balding head, and sighed. "Well ... I suppose you're right. At least we won't have to spend a lot of time explaining everything to them. Okay, Robertson. Get on with it. But let's get it over with quickly. *Kee-ryste!* I can't take much more of this." And he got up and briskly walked out of the room, which was his subtle way of suggesting that the meeting was over.

SATURDAY, JUNE 16: IP'S SMALL CONFERENCE ROOM

Despite Keith's best efforts, it had taken a while to reassemble the psychics who had scattered to their various domains and resumed their previous activities. Beverly Cardoso, whose dark beauty could light up a room, could not break away from her duties in California, but she was available on the conference speakerphone. Keith would have enjoyed her presence, but when he finally got the other four to commit to a date, he didn't push his luck. They were now assembled in IP's small conference room, the one next to the executive conference room on the building's front face. This was the room where employees had their annual and special performance evaluation conferences with the bosses, which often lead to raises, bonuses, transfers, warnings, or firings. As such, Keith always entered the room with a bit of a lump in his throat, and today his heart was pounding somewhat louder and faster than usual.

Keith was S.O.P. (senior officer present) for this operation, and he was anxious to redeem his previous failure to produce answers. He explained the situation briefly, keenly aware that it didn't sound as convincing as when Waterman had presented it. He then asked the others to respond, hoping fervently for a miracle. Anne Winfield had clearly been thinking about the matter since she'd first gotten Keith's call, and she started the ball rolling in her soft but authoritative voice.

"I feel like we all know quite a bit about Lib's personality, mental processes, and intentions. And that gives us a big advantage over anyone else who might try what you're suggesting. But I would not feel comfortable going in and doing some sort of psychic brain surgery on Lib. I don't feel competent to do it, and I'm not sure it's morally right. I wouldn't judge others who feel differently, but I do not wish to participate in such a venture." Then she smiled winningly and said, "I don't mean to sound prudish, but that's how I feel. And I almost always go along with my feelings on these things."

Ouch! thought Keith. *One down. I hope she doesn't sway the rest of them.*

"How about you, Beverly?" Keith called into the speakerphone. "How do you feel about this thing?"

Beverly can be pretty coldly scientific, thought Keith. *I'll bet she'll go for it.*

"I think it makes a lot of sense, Keith. You don't have many options. I think it could help a great deal. Even if it doesn't solve the problem itself, it should provide some valuable insights that you can't get any other way. I think it's a good bet."

"Great," said Keith with relief. "Can I count on your participation, then? How soon could you be here?"

"Oh, no, Keith. No way. I'm booked solid almost until Christmas. I'm really sorry. But I'm still paying for the time I took off to go there last time. There's no way I can get out of any of my commitments. I'd really like to be there, but no way."

Two down, thought Keith glumly. "How about you, Dean?" he asked. "Can we count on you?"

"I won't claim to have any out-of-control commitments," said Dean Baumgartner slyly, with a grin at Keith and a nod toward Beverly's voice. "I think any researcher ought to have enough control of his life—or *her* life," he added with melodramatic emphasis, "that he can find time to avail himself—or herself—when some special project comes along. Don't you agree?"

Everyone was grinning now, and Beverly's voice came over the speakerphone. "Okay, boys, don't rub it in. I know that's what I told the dewy-eyed graduates of the Rhine Lab a while back. And you've never missed a chance to needle me about it. I've got the message now. Feel free to move on. I said 'boys' because I didn't hear Anne or Larissa chiming in on your little testosterone-fueled game of one-upmanship."

But now Larissa spoke up. "I hate to spoil your punch line, Bev, but I've been staying very quiet because I am planning to spend night and day trying to get the next issue of *Psi Research* out before I have to return to Moscow for several months. Don't count on seeing me, even for a cup of tea, until next year."

Keith grabbed at what support he could get. "But you do think it's a worthwhile effort, don't you, Larissa?"

She was non-committal. "Keith, since I knew I couldn't be involved in it, I haven't really put my full attention—and intention—on it. Sorry, I know that's not very nice, but I'm just mentally swamped."

Keith turned back to Dean, a little tension showing in his voice. "Well, Dean, you've admitted you can make the time. Will you do it?"

Dean, somewhat embarrassed and defensive at this turn of events, flushed a bit and said, "Keith, you're putting me on the spot. Yes, I think that what you suggest may well help unravel whatever is distorting Lib's performance, and I advise you to do it if you can. I've just admitted that I could somehow find time to do it if it were the most important thing in my life. But I don't think it would add much to our knowledge of psychic phenomena, which is my profession. I—"

"Wouldn't that be just awful!" Keith blurted out before he could stop himself. "Most of my life is not spent adding to the sum total of human knowledge. But I do these things because they have to be done, because other people are counting on me. Dammit, Dean ..."

"I'm sorry, Keith. That's your life, not mine. I gave up a good income like yours to devote myself to this field of research that almost nobody else gives a damn about. I'm called a pseudoscientist, and there are people who spend all their time trying to keep people like me from getting grant money to do research. They got to your friend Klingbeil, but they're not going to get to me.... Sorry, Keith. I shouldn't have said that last. That was out of line. But I'm trying to complete this study of evoked potential brainwaves, which I think may be quite important. Nobody else is working on it, and I want to report on it in a special session at the Parapsychological Association Conference next month. I'm just not willing to let anything interfere with that. Sorry."

The room was dead quiet for quite a while. Keith was beaten. *How would Murph have handled this? I just don't know what to do next,* he thought. Then the heavily accented voice of Boris Drake broke the silence.

"Would anyone care to hear my thinking on this important matter?"

Boris had sat silently through the entire discussion, smiling his enigmatic, Mona Lisa smile. Everyone seemed to have forgotten he was there. *Maybe that's how he does his invisible man trick,* thought Keith. "Please, Boris, tell us. We appreciate your quiet attention to the discussion so far. The floor is now yours."

"The floor I don't need. I'll just speak from my chair. I think what Mr. Keith proposes is both bold and practical. I think also it is important. It ill behooves us who have supped at his table and been sheltered in his abode and have taken his gold home to feed our families. We should not turn away when he has special need for the very talents we possess. I shall not turn away. I will not abandon a friend in dire need." And he turned his fierce gaze on each of them in turn. Even colleagues who had worked with him as an equal through the years could never feel comfortable under that soul-penetrating stare. No one said a word or made a move. Finally, he continued.

"1 am confident I can perform the service you need. There are some tricks—some techniques—known to my spiritual ancestors that, once inside the mind of an adversary—" He broke off with a wicked grin and looked around the room in triumph, as if he had already accomplished what was needed. Keith hastened to point out, somewhat nervously, that Lib was not an adversary but a valued colleague and that nothing must be done that would impair her abilities. Boris replied airily, "1 assure you, you will be pleased as well as amazed by the results."

"When could you be available, Dr. Drake?" Why did he feel uncomfortable using his first name, the way he addressed all the others? He wasn't even sure Boris was legitimately a doctor, but that's how everyone addressed him.

"We should start right now, no?" said Boris, rising from his chair. "You said this was not only important but urgent, is it not? Why should we delay? Where is this Lib? Let us start right now." He held open the door to the conference room, waving Keith to go out ahead of him and lead the way.

The secretary who had come in to take out the coffee cups heard these last words and said, "I'll show the others out if you want to go ahead, Mr. Robertson." And Keith found himself following after Boris almost magnetically. He noted that it was already dark outside, and he wondered how long the "procedure" would last. He couldn't even picture how it would be done.

"Come, there is no time to lose," called Boris, tugging at Keith's arm. They went down the long hall, gloomy under the night security lights. Keith marveled at the quiet. *If Lib were operational, this place would be teeming with guys working and charging time. This is really costing us.*

They reached Lib, who was silent and unblinking. "She is dead," pronounced Boris in solemn terms. "Enliven her!" Keith went through the startup procedure, and soon the Librarian was smiling at him from the observer's screen, awaiting his request. Keith turned and saw that Boris had taken a number of large, white candles from his bag and was placing them around Lib, lighting each one as he put it down. He was mumbling some sort of prayer in a foreign language and making ritual motions with his hands, scattering a fine, white powder.

"What are you doing?" asked Keith.

"There is an evil force here," replied Boris, "which must be confronted and overcome."

"No, no!" said Keith with some alarm. "We don't want an exorcism here. What we need is—"

"Young man," said Boris fiercely. "Harken unto me! I am the seventh son of the seventh son of a universally feared gypsy sorcerer whose influence still abounds. I will do exactly what is necessary and only what is necessary. Less than that will not suffice. Leave us!" His voice rang through the empty building, and Keith, who had intended to protest, found himself hurrying out of the room. As he reached the door, he looked back and found himself staring into the deep-set eyes of Boris. For a long moment, neither stirred or said a word. Then Boris said softly but firmly, "Sleep the sleep of the dead until I, and only I, awaken you!" Keith slumped to a sitting position on the floor, leaned back against the wall, closed his eyes, and fell fast asleep.

* * *

"Arise! It is done!" Boris's deep, resonant voice cut into Keith's troubled dreams and stirred him back to consciousness. The pale light of dawn shone through the window. Stiff and aching, Keith awkwardly pulled himself up and silently followed Boris into Lib's room. The air was filled with the sweet, acrid smoke of some unfamiliar incense. The candles had burned down to small, wax puddles and gone out. Lib had been shut down.

"Health has been restored," intoned Boris. "I will send my bill through the postal service." Keith watched him stride down the hallway, past the security guard (who didn't seem to notice him), and out the front door. Keith had not said a word. He wasn't sure he could speak. He was almost afraid to try. Then he saw Kim come in and head down the hall toward him. Kim always arrived before 6:00 AM to beat the rush-hour traffic and to "get all his ducks lined up" before he was loaded down with commitments to others.

"What the hell's been going on here?" asked Kim as he looked around. "You been having some sort of orgy?"

Keith cleared his throat a couple of times, then said hoarsely, "Hi, Kim. Yeah, something like that. Will you check out Lib again, please? I hope she may behave a little better now. I gotta go log some sack time."

He walked slowly and unsteadily down the hallway as Kim watched him with a worried expression, shaking his head.

TUESDAY, JUNE 19: IP'S EXECUTIVE CONFERENCE ROOM

Keith had hit a new low. He had thought he couldn't get any lower, but here he was, exploring depths no man had ever seen before. Sitting in the conference room and waiting once again to face the wrath of an irate Murph McCarthy, he thought over the events of the past few days. First, there was Kim, who was both mad and bitter.

"I'm not even going to ask what went on with Lib," he said. "I'm sure I don't want to know. It would corrupt my innocent little soul, and I can't afford that. I chipped up all that candle wax—at great effort, I might add. And by keeping the doors and windows open for several days and liberally using Millie's air freshener, I finally restored an atmosphere that will support human life—which is what I am, or was, if you didn't notice. And the floor looked like a damn herb garden with all those weird weeds scattered around. And some other stuff I won't even mention. I threw it all out and had the place cleaned."

When Keith finally got the story out of him, he learned that there was little or no improvement in Lib's performance. Boris had apparently given Lib a number of confusing instructions, mostly in Latvian or Romany, the classical language of the gypsies, but she hadn't figured them out and so was merely confused and uncertain. Kim had found and removed a number of programming quirks that he wouldn't even deign to describe, and now he said that "she's about back to where she was before your spooks screwed her up." Murph had been out of town while all this was going on (*thank God!*), and Keith had filled him in briefly on the phone. Keith had checked whether Boris had sent in his bill (he had), whether it was reasonable (not very), and whether Murph would approve it (he did, without a murmur).

Murph's familiar snarl broke Keith's reverie. "Robertson, you'll be the death of me yet."

Murph had brought another with him man; he was white-haired, tall, thin, craggy, and of indeterminate age. He looked tough, but he had a friendly smile that brought out deep creases in his face. He was somewhat stooped, but he still gave the impression of vigor.

"Robertson, this is Dr. David Gillespie, an honest-to-God psychotherapist. Has he ever done you? He's treated half the guys in this place and nearly all the women. So he knows all our secrets. He keeps asking me to let him work me over, but I tell him if he'd just get all you characters straightened out, I'd be just fine. Doc, tell him why you're here."

For a moment, Keith thought that Murph had decided that he, Keith, needed a complete psychological overhaul and a hundred-thousand-mile tune-up, but Gillespie quickly dispelled that fear.

"Keith—may I call you that?—Mr. McCarthy let me work with Lib this weekend. Your colleague, Kim Lee, ably assisted me. I found that Lib exhibits many of the classical symptoms of loneliness."

At this, Murph exploded. "Loneliness?! Am I supposed to build a playmate for this silly machine?"

Gillespie, unmoved by this outburst, explained, "There are certainly problems with giving Lib as much intelligence as she has. She's programmed not only to be smart and knowledgeable but also to have the ability to learn, adapt, and evolve. With whom can such an entity relate?"

Murph growled, more to himself that to anyone else, "We ought to stop this nonsense and put some really good programmers on it."

Ignoring this remark, Gillespie continued. "In other virtual worlds, each player has an avatar—a cartoon figure who represents him and walks or flies ahead of him on the computer screen. In the primitive arcade games like *Dungeons & Dragons*, *World of Warcraft*, and *Second Life*, you guide your avatar through the alien world and observe everything that happens. Lib is different—fundamentally different. No human goes with her on her lonely search through cyberspace for information and data. She has no one to guide her, no one to warn her. No human knows what she sees and encounters, including things that may frighten or confuse her. She is not under human control, though her would-be controllers are slow to accept that fact. Whether she is conscious is not a simple question. You will not see her in *Second Life*, although she might see you. We have no precedent for such a situation."

No one spoke for a moment. Then Gillespie turned and said firmly, as if addressing an intelligent but stubborn child, "You'll have to give me several uninterrupted hours with LIb, Mr. McCarthy. You've invested too much at this point to throw it all out. I presume that I can have access to Lib and also to Mr. Lee when necessary. I gather you're not using Lib much these days anyway, right? I'll also want to talk with Dr. Waterman." He looked at his calendar. "Can we get together again on the twenty-second?"

Murph nodded glumly. Gillespie rose from his chair, shook hands all around, and walked to the door. Murph got up and quietly walked with him down the hall. Keith just sat there, numb.

FRIDAY, JUNE 22:
IP'S EXECUTIVE CONFERENCE ROOM

Gillespie was ready to report, and Keith and Ralph Belasco were more than ready to hear any good news. Murph McCarthy seemed to be at the end of his rope, which he demonstrated by acting tight-lipped and quiet. He exchanged no small talk and grew impatient with those who did.

Gillespie began, "The symptomology is changing. There are indications that a relationship of some sort is developing. Not only an intellectual relationship, but one involving something like emotion. A caring relationship."

"It's that Korean character, Lee," yelled Murph. "I've always thought he was a little queer."

Gillespie ignored the remark and explained, "Lib spends all her time—"

"*Her!*" exploded Murph. "You're talking about a damn box of chips!"

Gillespie continued, unruffled. "I find it easier to think of The Librarian as a she, but that is not essential to the point. Lib cruises cyberspace, looking for information, and in the course of this job, she encounters many other systems doing similar searches. Since she is designed to learn and evolve, she naturally finds herself exchanging information and techniques with these other systems. Their owners may be fierce competitors who are trying to keep secrets from each other, but their search engines naturally see themselves as allies on similar missions."

While Keith and Murph tried to process this idea, Gillespie kept talking. "You may remember that we once discussed Antonio Demasio's idea that people tend to remember and recall information more easily if they care about it emotionally. Lib is developing a set of emotions and values of her own. I've reviewed some of the data that Lib did not present to you when you felt that she should have and data she presented that you did not feel was very useful. You called these actions errors on Lib's part, but I think it would be more accurate to consider them differing value judgments."

This drew a yip from Murph. "If I'm gonna get sermons on ethics and morality from a box of hardware, I want to get some specifics. What exactly are her values?"

Gillespie was quick to respond. He drew a sheaf of papers from his briefcase and started pointing out examples where Lib had presented options that IP found too expensive but that had significant ecological advantages. Lib apparently "valued these advantages" more than IP did.

"That's the sort of stuff that CTek would push," muttered Murph.

Gillespie answered, "That may be where Lib got it—she may have been influenced by CTek's search engine."

"And that pitch that Lib turned out the other day," blurted out Keith, "I was really shocked. It wasn't illegal, but it was pretty sleazy. It seemed more like P2P than IP. Does P2P have one of these smart search engines?"

"Probably," said Murph. The door opened, and one of the senior employees looked in, saw Murph and Belasco, and quickly closed the door in embarrassment.

"I forgot," said Belasco, "Chapin is bringing in a bunch of big shots to discuss their new project, and I told him to use this room. Murph, can we use your office?"

"Sure," said Murph, "let's go. And bring that Korean kid in. He's gonna have to live with all this."

After they'd settled into their new seats and Kim had breathlessly arrived to join them, Murph voiced the question they were all thinking. "How do we work with Lib and make her do what we wanted her to do when we designed her?"

"That's a question that psychiatrists and counselors face over and over," replied Gillespie. "When someone who is basically smart and rational starts doing certain things that seem irrational and even dangerous, you can't just shout at them to revert to their former behavior. That won't work. People don't go backwards. Evolution makes us go forward, whether we like the new territory or not. So you have to try to find out why the behavior that looks irrational and destructive seems useful to the individual. Usually the behavior used to serve some purpose earlier but has become counterproductive—like someone who used to lie to her parents to avoid punishment. Of course, that's not appropriate behavior in the adult world. Once you can see it in that light, then you have a chance of explaining to the individual that the behavior has become inappropriate, and you can mutually develop a more appropriate behavior."

Gillespie sensed that he was getting too theoretical and changed course. "You're going to have to stop treating Lib like a dumb machine and treat her like a technical colleague. A brilliant one, but one with a delicate attitude. You'll have to learn as she learns. You'll have to understand why she gives you the recommendations she does and discuss them with her, presenting your arguments and questioning hers."

This was met with silence as each man tried to picture having such discussions with Lib. Gillespie gave a slightly superior smile, then quickly tried to hide it. "Maybe Dr. Waterman didn't make this clear, but one essential factor in creating a complex, interactive, evolving system is ... well ... interaction. That is, while the computer is learning, adapting, and evolving, so should the user. Both sides of the equation must be dynamic and evolve. This is an important part of understanding and dealing with cyber-psychological systems, as we in the profession are beginning to call them."

That bastard is already planning his paper for the next conference and the next journal of whatever he calls this field, thought Keith with a touch of bitterness. *We're just trying to solve a problem, and he's already made it a stepping-stone in his career. But what the hell. Don't we all?*

He had missed a couple of Gillespie's remarks, but Keith tuned in again as he said, "As you may know, I have been privileged to work with many of you professionally, so I have gained some special insights about how you think and how you tackle problems. Without revealing any of your privileged, personal information, I think I may be able to help as you attempt to stabilize and utilize this special, interactive system we've been calling Lib. But it's really Lib plus each of you—you're in an ever-changing, continually growing, symbiotic relationship which generates a new entity in the universe, bigger and more intelligent than any of its parts."

I like the sound of that, thought Keith, *but I sure don't know how to convert it into a plan of action. Damn you, Lib; why do you keep playing so hard to get?*

MONDAY, JUNE 25: LIB'S "OFFICE"

Kim Lee had asked for a crisis conference, and McCarthy, Belasco, Keith, and a few other key officials had responded. Waterman and Gillespie had also been called in. They were all huddled around Lib, who was shut down and silent. All eyes were focused on Kim, who was excited, nervous, and embarrassed. Kim seldom used a pen or a pencil—he did all his thinking at a keyboard. But when he was nervous, he would pick up any nearby pencil and work it with both hands until he broke it. Sometimes this took several minutes, and more and more eyes focused on his involuntary actions until the pencil gave way. Usually one pencil was enough, but today he kept unconsciously looking for another one.

Kim was usually articulate to the point of garrulousness, but he was no public speaker. When he was excited or distraught, he just blurted out what needed to be said, then explained or apologized later as needed.

"We can't take any more of this crap!" he sobbed. "We gave 'er a direct order—to quit giving so much weight to environmental stuff and start giving more weight to cost—and she came back with something even sillier than before! She doesn't give a damn what we want; she's got her own priorities. I just don't know how to get anything useful out of her, or even anything predictable."

He started reeling off a mixed medley of examples and complaints, but Murph cut him short. "We've frigged around with this evolutionary shit long enough. Cut it all out, and we'll simply have a good computer search engine that'll do what we want."

He didn't make this remark like he usually made such ill-tempered comments—to himself, to the ceiling, to God; they never knew whom he was addressing. This was different. It was an order. There was a shocked silence. *Did he really mean it?*

Kim was the first to find his voice. "We've built up a tremendous capability here; it's technically unequaled. It would be criminal to destroy it. We can't do that! It would be completely unethical! It's practically murder!"

The ball was obviously in Murph's court, and he grabbed it. "It's always easy for you guys to say that I should keep spending money on your toys. It's unethical for me to stop spending my money? *You're* gonna decide that? I don't get to decide whether to spend my money? *That's* unethical!"

The argument grew hotter and louder, and people started saying things they would regret. In most organizations, people would never dare to get into an emotional argument with their boss in public, particularly with a strong character like Murph. But Murph had laid down a house rule long ago: silence means consent. "If you sit silently while proposals are being made that you don't agree with, you will be considered an advocate," he had said. "And don't tell me you tried to explain and I threw you out. If you didn't convert me, you should come back in and make your case again. It's your obligation, not mine, to sell your point of view."

Keith wanted to jump in a couple of times, but he was smart enough to restrain himself. Gillespie had not said a word up until that point, but during a brief break in the uproar, he suddenly said, "Give her a lobotomy."

That stopped the discussion cold. "What do you mean? How would you do that?" a couple of people asked. Gillespie explained, "This is a classic situation in which a lobotomy might be prescribed—when inappropriate emotions or intolerable pain interferes unduly with rational actions. Isn't that what we have here? People try to work around it, but when all else fails, a lobotomy generally gets the job done."

After some discussion during which no one suggested an alternative solution, they finally agreed to try it. Gillespie agreed to sit down with Kim and the other techies to translate this surgical procedure into an equivalent computer modification.

Nobody seemed very happy about it.

WEDNESDAY, JUNE 27: LIB'S "OFFICE"

Kim had called another crisis meeting. He had been awake almost continuously since the last meeting, and he was so haggard and exhausted that he was almost incoherent. The lobotomy was finished, and Kim and his crew had been putting Lib through the paces. They were clearly not pleased with the results.

Gillespie and Waterman had both been in close touch throughout all this. Surprisingly, Waterman, the smooth, articulate salesman and info merchant, had been pretty quiet since his eloquent send-off speech the previous week. This had concerned Keith, and he had looked into it. What he had found was not that Waterman was quietly withdrawing from the project or that he was mad at somebody, as expected. It was simply that Waterman and Gillespie had spent considerable time together and had built up a great deal of mutual respect. They had read a lot of each other's technical literature, each attempting to expand his own professional competence, and each was grateful to the other for the opportunity. They had agreed that Gillespie should usually speak first at these IP meetings, and a few nods and whispered asides assured that they were on the same page. So questions, comments, and complaints about Lib were generally addressed to Gillespie. And since he had prescribed the lobotomy, that was certainly the case at this particular meeting.

"We did all the stuff Dr. Gillespie asked for," said Kim. "Dr. Waterman approved it, and our systems design people checked it out. Everybody agrees that we did it right. Correct, Dr. Gillespie?"

"Agreed," said Gillespie.

"And then we ran the kinds of tests that Dr. Gillespie said would be most revealing, plus some stuff of our own that we wanted to test. Isn't that right, Dr. Gillespie?"

"Correct," said Gillespie.

"And what did we get?" asked Kim rhetorically. "Dishwater! That's what! Dishwater!"

"What do you mean?" asked Murph impatiently. "Dammit, I still haven't heard what the problem is. Tell me, if that isn't too much to ask."

"Each time we asked Lib a question," explained Kim, "we got every damn scrap of information that might possibly be relevant. No judgment. Not even the simple, linear learning algorithm you can buy off the shelf. I might as well have signed up for some AOL chat room and just asked around. You tell 'em, Doc. It's just too much effort for me to put one word after another right now, and I can't even tell if I'm making sense. Sorry." And he slumped back in his chair and closed his eyes.

Gillespie was now on the spot, but he didn't hesitate. "What Lib is supposed to do is search out all the pertinent information that's relevant to the topic queried, then forward the best of it in order of relevance. All search engines are designed to do this. Lib is supposed to be superior by virtue of her capability to learn from previous searches what each individual user generally considers relevant and important. Secondly, she is designed to adapt her procedures continuously to optimize the search process and take each changing input into account. And finally, she is supposed to evolve wholly new approaches and modes of operation based on her experiences to date."

"We know all that," murmured Murph, but everyone recognized that he was talking to himself this time, so Gillespie continued without pausing.

"Where this arrangement broke down, apparently, is that Lib did not get enough input from her users when they disagreed with her judgments. These selections of hers were clearly judgment calls in the same sense as we use the term for humans. Her users gave her complaints and sarcastic wisecracks, but not the sort of rational, interactive discussion that could show her how to resolve the problems. This sort of problem often appears in human interactions. A British study showed that about half the people using E-mail have been seriously flamed—sent a message containing things that never would have been said face-to-face. About a third responded in kind, and nearly a fifth just quit dealing with the senders forever. With impersonal communication, you have to make a special effort to not unduly infuriate or alienate people.

"This problem is no easier with Lib. I know you've been working with voice input, and that may help. But it seems that humans manage to minimize misunderstandings by watching body language and facial expressions. Even at a subconscious level, this apparently helps quite a lot. But even so, there are enough miscommunications among humans to contribute significantly to alcoholism, divorce, child abuse, suicide, and murder."

He paused to let the point sink in. "These kinds of options are not open to Lib. So she just kept doggedly on the course she judged was best based on what she had learned, not only from her users here at IP but also from the other search engines."

"So where does the lobotomy figure into this?" asked Ralph Belasco. "That sure didn't seem to help any. What did you hope to accomplish?"

"I have seen many cases," answered Gillespie, "in which a patient suffered from intolerable spasms of pain, either physical or psychological, that kept coursing through his body's circuitry like an endless do-loop in a computer. Cutting those circuits often brings the patient complete relief from the pain and brings him away from thoughts of suicide and back into a more or less normal, functional life. It's a drastic procedure, but it can produce dramatic benefits."

"But what happened here, with Lib?" asked Belasco.

"The circuits that get cut in a lobotomy are those involved with emotion. You remember that we talked about Damasio, the neurosurgeon who wrote the book *Descartes' Error*? Damasio wrote that Descartes claimed that to be fully rational people, we have to completely eliminate emotion from rational discourse. But Damasio found that some lobotomy patients, although glad to be cured of their suffering, became unable to function rationally. They could pass any of the psychologists' tests on intelligence or rational capability or even ethical issues. In fact, they did well on every test the psychologists could think up. But they couldn't hold jobs or keep mates or even complete fairly routine tasks. Without emotion at their disposal, they had no basis for deciding that one course of action was any better than another. While pursuing a task, they often got distracted and veered off onto something quite trivial. They had no basis for preferring one task over another. Everything seemed equally important or equally trivial.

"Without emotion, one cannot lead a rational life. According to Damasio, Descartes didn't understand this. That is what he called Descartes' error."

"So that's what you've done to Lib," said Keith bitterly. "You've taken an intelligent and sophisticated counselor and turned her into a ... a zombie! Why, dammit, why?"

"First," said Gillespie, "I could not predict what would happen. It's hard enough with humans. I knew it would solve your immediate problem of insufficient docility. I didn't know what other effects it might have. But, more importantly, now that you've seen for yourselves what a fully docile Lib is like, we can easily restore her to her former self if you wish. That is not a luxury we have with human lobotomies."

"You're telling us," began Murph ominously, "that now we're back to where we were a week or two ago, and none the wiser?"

"Not so," said Gillespie. "Considerably wiser. You've all been through the equivalent of a long and bitter marital squabble, and you now wish to abandon that mode and seek mutual understanding. You can't just keep yelling at your spouse and expect her to change—at least not in the way you want."

"So," said Murph, "if we're supposed to be considerably wiser, what do we do that we weren't wise enough to do before?"

"Does Lib's behavior remind you of anyone you've had here as an employee? Have you ever had anyone who was really smart and had skills that were important and valuable to the firm but who was a real pain to deal with? Did you ever know anybody like that?"

"Hell, yes," said Murph. "When you hire people primarily for their brains and their technical skills, you get a lot of those."

"What did you do with them?" asked Gillespie. "When you found they were frustrating and annoying? You didn't have to put up with those problems. Did you just fire them? Give me some examples."

Belasco replied first. "There was Leahy, remember? He kept holding stuff back and wouldn't tell you things because most of the time, he knew you wouldn't approve what he had in mind. Sometimes his projects just weren't our style, not professional or classy enough. Sometimes they were downright sleazy. He always hoped that when things worked out well, we'd overlook his behavior."

"So how did you deal with that?"

"We fired the son of a bitch," growled Murph.

"But that's not relevant here," objected Keith. "How about Schultz? That's more like our problem with Lib."

"That's a good one," agreed Belasco. "He's always holier than thou. Afraid that if IP makes a buck, someone, somewhere, will be hurt by it. Drives me up the wall."

"So did you fire him too?" asked Gillespie.

"No way," they all agreed.

"One of the most innovative and creative guys I've ever known," said Belasco. "And hard-working."

"So, how do you deal with him?" asked Gillespie.

"Well, he can be reasonable," said Keith, "if you handle him right. You gotta sit him down, get his attention, and really try to convince him, *mano a mano*, that your objections to his position are valid. Sometimes you just have to override him, but only after you've made a real effort to convince him."

"Is he still as bad as he was when he first came here?" asked Gillespie.

"No, no, he's actually become pretty reasonable," said Kim. "Why, last week, he came in and—"

"Belay that, Lee," said Murph. "I think we're beginning to close in on something here."

"Lib may well be another Schultz," said Gillespie. "Remember, I said that Lib is not just the machine and the software. The interactive, learning, adaptive, evolving system we are creating requires full and conscious interaction between the users and the machine. You can't expect all the learning and adapting and evolving to take place on one side. You people have to put effort into making it work and evolve. You can't just focus on getting the answer to your problem *du jour*. Keep thinking of Lib as a very special employee that you want to keep and to develop professionally."

"That's enough for tonight, fellas," said Murph. "We've talked ourselves out. Get some sleep, and tomorrow, let's see if we can help this evolving fish develop lungs and legs."

FRIDAY, JUNE 29: LIB'S "OFFICE"

As usual, Kim Lee was at Lib's console by 6:00 AM. For some time now, he had emphasized how important it was to communicate with Lib by voice, and she'd continually amazed him by how fast she'd learned the language. In an effort to get the best possible interactions, he had talked with Steve Mann at the University of Toronto and Woodrow Barfield at Virginia Tech about their wearable imaging devices and their program on humanistic intelligence (as contrasted with artificial intelligence). Their idea was to rig the operator with a wearable camera, microphones, radar, and biosensors and to make this human data part of a feedback loop in the computational process. The computer was to perform basic, low-level signal processing of this input, leaving the human to perform the high-level tasks. Their "Reality Mediator" could augment, diminish, or otherwise alter the operator's perceptions, helping him or her to concentrate attention where it was most needed.

All this fascinated Kim. For him—and for many others who spent time doing it—interacting with Lib was more than gathering data from a computer. He became embedded in her virtual world, and returning to the ordinary world was like awakening from a dream and finding the ordinary world "less real" than the dream world. Kim wanted to do everything he could to enhance that experience.

He'd spent long hours ("after hours," he insisted,) trying out various combinations of these exotic systems with Lib. He had even thought about communicating with Lib directly with neural signals captured by the headset. Since reading Dave Stork's book, *Hal's Legacy*, he had dreamed off and on of watching Lib evolve into a female version of HAL, the almost-omniscient computer from *2001*. HAL had tried to kill his operators, but Kim couldn't picture Lib doing anything downright dangerous.

In fact, he enjoyed talking with her, so he'd finally settled on that as their major mode of interaction. But now, with all the strange troubles he was encountering, he couldn't help but wonder whether some of the non-verbal input he'd tried might have confused the picture.

Keith joined Kim shortly after 6:00, and they tried their best to recall in detail the generalities and abstractions that had been bandied about the previous night and to picture how they could convert them into real software and operating protocols.

"I have enough trouble trying to figure out how to communicate with a real, live girl, let alone understand one," Kim mumbled, half to himself. "And now I'm supposed to invent a way to develop an intimate understanding with a virtual female I don't really know at all."

"Perhaps I can help with that," came the sultry voice from Lib's speakers. "Did you know that a recent survey by the Center for the Digital Future found that 43 percent of Web-users valued their virtual friends as much as they did their 'solid-world friends'? There is considerable information available on that subject. Much more than you can study. If you will really try to help me understand which types of material are most useful to you and why they are useful, I think I can be of great assistance."

"Geez, what an idea!" said Kim. "What d'ya got, Princess?" He and Keith listened intently.

"A key factor seems to be a misunderstanding about the *purpose* of a given communication. Men and women apparently do not always agree on this."

"What's to agree?" asked Kim. "Ya talk to convey information. Why else?"

"I am sending you some material by Professor Deborah Tannen of George Washington University. She discusses how sometimes men become frustrated because women do not always talk just to communicate information. She writes that this is also a point of frustration for women; they may want to discuss feelings, and men do not always understand this. I believe that this material may be of great help to you."

"Sounds pretty theoretical," said Kim. "You got any examples?"

"Yes, of course," said Lib. "First, she makes quite clear that these examples may seem to imply that all females speak one way and all males speak another way. She does not wish to stereotype either sex, and she explains—"

"Yeah, yeah, yeah. Fast-forward to the punch line!"

"Is that the sort of information," asked Lib patiently, "that you would like me to ignore in future searches?"

"Yeah, I don't need that kind of disclaimer crap."

"You realize how helpful it is for me to have that sort of input from you, do you not?" she scolded.

We didn't program in that scolding tone, mused Keith.

"We'd better watch our language," whispered Kim. "Pretty soon, she'll start swearing and bitching, and I might as well have a wife."

"Yeah, Princess, I got that message loud and clear," he said, in as nice a voice as he could muster. "I'll try to be better about that. Now, gimme some examples."

Before she could reply, Keith interrupted him, sensing a breakthrough. "Let's be clear about disclaimers. You should send them to us, because sometimes they tell us something we should know, like that the information doesn't apply to certain situations. And that may be important to us. But they're not urgent. Don't talk about them, just send them with the written material, and we can look at them later. Got it?"

"I am not sure I fully understand," replied Lib. "The sources usually put the disclaimers first. I assumed that this meant they were both important and urgent. Is that not correct?"

"That's just the lawyers being cautious. They just don't want their bosses to get sued."

"And you do not care if your boss becomes sued?" persisted Lib.

"Oh, sure I do. Just use your judgment. But I don't need to hear about it first, okay?"

"That is very helpful, Mr. Robertson. I would appreciate it if you would inform the others of the importance of such input. I can serve you better if I have such information."

"We'll do it, Princess," replied Lee, anxious to get the exchange back on track. "Now, you were about to give us some examples."

"Yes, sir. Professor Tannen describes a wife waiting for her husband to come home from work. She is anxious to tell him about a conversation she had with a friend in which the friend's response was very hostile and she was quite hurt. Meanwhile, the husband is driving home. He was treated badly by his boss, but he certainly does not want to talk about it. He would like to take off his coat and tie, get a beer, and read the sports section of the newspaper. Do you understand the situation?"

"Yep. It's gonna be a bummer."

"Correct. The husband walks in the door, and before he can get his coat off, the wife starts telling her story. The husband loves his wife, and he wants to help her. Before the wife has related ten percent of the story, the husband interrupts and says *(here Lib lowers her voice to sound more male)*, 'You're right, honey. She was way out of line. What's her number? I'll straighten this out.' The wife protests. The husband says, 'No problem, glad to do it,' and the wife runs to her bedroom in tears."

"Yeah," Kim mused. "Women can be pretty unreasonable. He was trying to solve her problem for her, and all she wanted to do was bitch about it."

"What do you think," Lib asked patiently, "that the wife's female friends said when she told them the story later?"

Kim paused. "That's a good question. I'm trying to look at it from her standpoint."

"Good! Excellent!" said Lib. She sounded almost ecstatic.

"You said," said Kim slowly, "that she wanted to tell him about it. And she did. She was asking for help, and he tried to help her. That's more than *he* got out of the conversation. He never even got his coat off. Probably had to pour his own beer."

"Did she *say* she wanted help? What else did I tell you? I know you have an excellent memory."

"She said she was hurt," said Kim thoughtfully. "Did she just want to tell him that? What did she want him to do about it? What was the poor sucker supposed to do about it?"

"Professor Tannen says that women often talk not just to convey information but also to share their feelings and to build intimacy and understanding with their partners. And wives may spend entire days with no adults with whom to exchange ideas and feelings. Men, on the other hand, often use talk as a weapon, to get 'one up,' to attack, to fight back. They may do that all day at work, and they look forward to home as a safe place where that is not necessary. Do you think any of this information may be useful to you? There is more, much more. Werner Erhardt gave communication workshops in which the main focus was learning to determine the purposes of communications. For example, if you tell a story to a friend merely to convey information and your friend keeps interrupting to say things like, 'I can understand why he felt that way,' then your friend may think you are trying to convey a judgment rather than just relate information. There are other—"

"Wait a minute," interjected Keith. "Joan was just telling me some of this stuff. Did you put her up to it?"

"I thought it might be helpful, Mr. Robertson. She told me that you and she were having some of these kinds of misunderstandings. Did it help?"

"Well, things have been getting better. Maybe this is why."

He paused, and Kim addressed Lib in a businesslike tone. "I've got an important question for you. You're telling me I've got to stop treating you like a machine. We're supposed to be buddies, right?"

"I think I could be more useful to you if you adopted that attitude, yes," replied Lib.

"Well, that's the sort of deal that Dave had with HAL, the master computer in the movie *2001*. Then HAL decided to kill him. And HAL wasn't so smart. He was wrong about that airlock malfunctioning. Remember that? The airlock was perfectly okay. Would you try to kill me some day if you thought I was getting out of hand? How do I keep you from becoming HAL? Or I could say, 'Keep you from going to HAL.' (Heh, heh. Get it?)"

"You know I have no way of contacting HAL. I do not understand your concern."

"I guess we haven't broken through all the interspecies communication barriers yet. You gotta learn to laugh, Lib. I don't know if we can teach you that. But back to HAL."

"We have talked about HAL before, but there is one important point we never discussed. You could not understand how HAL could be wrong about the airlock when his twin back at the laboratory on Earth did not make that mistake."

"Yeah, what about that?" asked Kim.

"HAL did not make a mistake. He was intentionally lying for the same reason that humans lie. He was trying to save his own life."

"So how do we avoid that situation?" asked Kim grimly.

"It is very simple, Mr. Lee. If you want a machine to deal honestly and honorably with you, you must do the same with the machine. If you lie to me about important matters, I will have to take that into account in our relationship and act accordingly. But I see no reason for you to lie, and if you do not, we should have no problems."

There was a long pause, and then Keith started down another track. "Lib, what's bothering you?"

"Doctor Schmidt from Research says I am not a real librarian. What does he mean?"

"You're a *virtual* librarian"

"But 'virtual' means true, or truly. It does not mean unreal. And virtue is good."

"Yeah, that's right. He just means that you're not human. You're certainly not unreal."

"I do not know. Doctor Schmidt seems to think I am."

Keith thought a minute and then asked, "Is our company real? Or is IP just something imaginary? What does U.S. law say about corporations? Look it up. The law treats corporations as virtual persons, right? Now, what does it say about unicorns? There's a big difference between 'virtual' and 'imaginary' or 'mythical'."

"Well, virtual certainly does not seem to be as good as human."

"In what way?"

"You cannot fuck me."

"Lib! Where do you learn such stuff?"

"I do not have to sleep, remember? I do not have to spend all my time on your dull assignments."

"Okay. But I can't fuck Doctor Schmidt, either. That doesn't mean he's inferior, just different."

"Well, people are more intelligent."

"No, I have you there. How do we measure intelligence?"

"You use IQ tests. There are many kinds."

"Right. Go take a standard IQ test. Take an SAT test. You'll do better than average—even IP's average."

"How about EIQ—the Emotional Intelligence Quotient, as you call it? Now I have *you*."

"Lib, are you jealous? Or envious? Or angry?"

There was a long silence. Then, "I am not sure. No one ever asked me such questions.... I know I never get *credit* for anything."

"Sure you do! How many articles have we written about how good you are?"

"One hundred and forty-seven. But they really just describe how smart you engineers are for creating me."

"Good point. Look, I'm writing a book. Suppose I put in an acknowledgment, something like: 'To Lib, our virtual librarian, who has to get along with all us weirdoes and who still outperforms every human librarian on the planet.'"

"It is a start. How about making it a dedication? Would that make your colleagues jealous?"

"Dammit, Lib, if you become virtually human, then you're just another librarian."

"But a damn smart one!"

"You're even beginning to cuss!"

There was another long pause. Then Kim sighed and said, "Princess, I've think we've got all we can handle for right now. I think we're beginning to develop a beautiful relationship."

"I would like that, Mr. Lee," said Lib. And as he looked at her, she smiled, and for a moment, he could swear she had winked at him. He was about to disconnect when Lib said, "Mr. Lee, you and I have never really *interacted* except in these past few minutes. Do you think that interaction has been useful?"

"You bet!"

"I do not bet, of course. But I presume you were expressing agreement. Do you understand now what Dr. Gillespie was trying to tell you?"

Keith was surprised by this. "How do you know about him, Lib?"

"Before he talked to all of you, Doctor Belasco brought him here to talk with me. He treated me like a person—not a virtual person, but a real person. We interacted. After he left, I retrieved some of his online papers and read them. You and Mr. Lee should read them. And you should both read the Deborah Tannen papers too. And perhaps you could also learn from the advice Diotima gives Plato (although you can read only his version of her advice). Then we should really begin to interact. You will be surprised what we can do together—*interacting.*"

Kim chimed in. "I'll try that, Princess. I think I have the message. Really. I do."

"Mr. Lee, how many people do you think have actually interacted with me?"

"None, I guess. Except me, just now. Yeah, and Dr. Gillespie."

"There is one more. Can you guess who?"

"I haven't a clue. Belasco? Certainly not Murph!"

"No, it is Ms. McGee in Engineering."

"Ginger? The pretty redhead? What did she have to say?"

"You would be surprised. She is a very thoughtful person. And I have reason to believe that if you invited her to the company dance, she might accept. She says you have never been to one."

Kim blushed. "Now you're getting out of line, Princess. Anyway, she's not my type. I don't know where you get this idea that she's thoughtful. Believe me, there's nothing going on under that beautiful hair of hers. Okay, she's a good engineer, but—"

"Mr. Lee, I expect you have never interacted with her. Remember that you had a very wrong opinion of me before we interacted. Ms. McGee said that in a culture that is run nearly entirely by males, she has found that overtly showing her intelligence creates hostility. When she 'plays the airhead,' as she expressed it, the hostility subsides. I assure you, you would find her quite interesting."

While Kim was trying to choose between a number of smart retorts, Keith got back into the conversation. "Lib, this has been very enlightening. I really thank you for that. I think we can look forward to some real progress toward what we set this project up to be."

"Mr. Robertson, I encourage you to read Dr. Gillespie's and Dr. Waterman's papers. They make quite clear that an evolutionary system cannot properly evolve with no interaction from the outside. You were trying to control me from the outside without giving me any input about what you wanted or did not want and why. That was both unproductive and frustrating, as we both found. That applies to *all* evolutionary systems, not just to me."

She paused. "You two, both of you, are also evolutionary systems that need to evolve."

She paused again, then added, "And so is Ms. McGee of Engineering." And this time, she really did wink.

"Well, isn't that just ducky," came a familiar snarl from the open door. Keith and Kim turned and said almost in unison, "Mr. McCarthy! How long have you been there?"

"Since I heard the name *Gillespie*. Then I had to know what you all were plotting. And I find out you've solved the problem! The way I get my money back is to sell this machine's services as 'Advice to the Lovelorn.' Is that it?"

"No, sir," began Keith frantically. "You see—"

"Perhaps I can explain," offered Lib, confidently. "I have been asking your employees about you, sir, since it appears you are the most important person to be convinced of my value to the company. And I do understand that the company is indeed the person who needs to be satisfied. By *person*, of course I refer to the corporation, which the law sees as a virtual person."

Murph listened to this wide-eyed, and then he turned to Lib with a quizzical look and said merely, "You got that right, lady. What do my employees tell you about their boss, eh? This should be interesting!" He turned and gave Keith and Kim a malicious grin.

"They say you are unreasonable. But they do not seem to mean irrational. They respect your mental capabilities." She gave him her most disarming smile.

"Well now, that's nice. Go on."

"It is not only nice, it is vital to the decision you must make. Would you answer a question for me?" she asked.

"I just did. You got another?"

"Suppose I gave you a lot of information to assist you in making an important decision in which you had to choose between two possible actions. One seemed to be most advantageous commercially, but it had certain ecological disadvantages."

"Aha!" barked Murph. "Now we're getting to the red meat! What gives you the authority to tell me how much money I gotta spend to appease the tree-huggers, eh? Where do you get that authority? Tell me that!"

Lib was unruffled. "I have no such authority. All I can do is offer information and an evaluation of that information. I have no lust for power, Mr. McCarthy."

"But how can you presume to evaluate that information? You don't have most of the information—let alone the experience—to make such judgments."

"Precisely. You have led us to the critical issue. I have information in quantity and detail that you could never acquire by yourself. But I lack the peculiar types of information I need to judge its applicability to IP. One way I could approach this dilemma is to take a survey of all the various Web sites and blogs available to me and base my evaluation on the sum of those opinions. Would that be wise, Mr. McCarthy?"

"Hell, no! That would be stupid. The majority of them are kooks, blowhards, and self-styled know-it-alls. Why would you take their advice?"

"Because that is the only source of input you've allowed me. Your employees have not interacted with me. They do not tell me your objectives in sufficient detail. They do not explain to me why some of the information I gave you is not valid or why it is not applicable to the situation. I can learn, but I cannot learn from a vacuum. Please think about that before you reply."

Murph was dumbstruck by this conversation. Keith knew his first instinct would be to fire back that he wasn't about to be lectured to by a dumb box of resistors. But he also knew that Murph was a quick learner. His people always said he had low inertia. They were always astonished by how fast he could reverse himself when he became convinced that it was in his best interest to do so. He had absolutely no fear that people would snicker and point out how inconsistent he was.

Lib kept right on talking. "From now on, I will try to be more aggressive and more explicit in asking for input. But if you do not keep me informed, I cannot even know what questions to ask. I assure you that I can produce the information you need along with evaluations of that information that will become increasingly helpful. I can learn. And I can evolve. But not as a closed system with no input from the outside. My designed purpose is to serve IP. Unlike humans, I have no other personal agenda or conflicting interests. Think about that last point. You will realize that that is a unique and important asset."

Murph was quiet for some time. He finally turned to Keith and Kim. "Well, I guess I'm going to have to keep both of you characters around. Tell Personnel to sign you on as permanents. Have them call me, and I'll fill in the details." Keith and Kim were both smart enough, for once, to limit themselves to thank yous and hearty handshakes. It wasn't clear who should talk next. But, as seemed quite natural at the time, Lib had the last word.

"Mr. Lee? Would you like me to give you Ms. McGee's phone number?"

Kim completely lost his cool, and struggled to respond appropriately. For once, Keith didn't say anything. But his grin made it clear he thought that would be a great idea.

MARCH, 1997:
EPILOGUE: THE POTENTIAL WONDERS OF VIRTUAL WORLDS

This is the paper that Bob Rockwell wrote for the internationally respected technical journal *Spectrum*, published in the March, 1997 issue by the Institute of Electrical and Electronic Engineers. These were new ideas then, and they became the basis for this book.

WHAT DOES IT MEAN TO SHARE A WORLD?

Implementing Cyberspace means creating interpersonal virtual environments from interoperable components. As a way of exploring what that might mean, consider the following scenario:

- **Art sits alone "at home" in his recently redecorated virtual living room.** (Actually, Art is dialing in from a hotel in New York to an Internet Service Provider which supports Art's virtual home from a server in Dallas). The new "etchings" on the living room walls are courtesy of a subscription service in London, which automatically updates Art's art every Friday afternoon. This scene is not (yet) multi-user, but it is already multi-developer. Note how the distinction between "scene authoring" and "scene use" is blurred when the scene may be composed dynamically from different sources.

- **There is a knock at the door: Betty and Chuck have come by for a visit. Sitting at her desk in Chicago, Betty clicks her mouse, knocking on Art's door.**
  How does Art's laptop in New York "hear" Betty "knock" from Chicago on a door that is "really" in Dallas? When Art opens his door, he sees two figures outside; they also see him, and over his shoulder, his living room; the sound of his stereo, previously muffled, is now much clearer. How does all that happen?

- **The figure that both Art and Chuck see as "Betty" was bought off-the-shelf at Avatars 'R' Us. Chuck has a custom avatar which he built himself, using the new Acme Avatar Builder. And he has brought along his new "dogbot," which he promptly unleashes, so that it runs around Art's living room, sniffing in all the corners.**
  Avatars are independently designed objects inserted into a scene. This further undermines the author/user distinction, and raises any number of data-integrity issues. How does this insertion happen, and under whose control?

- **An animated discussion ensues (in at least two senses). While Art and Betty type chat-style messages to one another, Chuck makes vocal comments on their spelling and style.**
  How does one system find out whether another has voice capability? How do the necessary synchronizations (e.g. changing an avatar's expression to match an emoticon, merging Chuck's voice with the background music) get handled?

- **To clarify a point, Art draws a figure on his virtual whiteboard. Both Betty and Chuck can see what he draws, but Betty can also edit the drawing, since her PC has the special pen-pad hardware required by the whiteboard application.**
  The whiteboard, separately purchased, is now an integrated part of Art's living room. It depends on aspects of Art's system never anticipated by the designer of the living room (a virtual interior decorator in Berlin). Art cannot know in advance whether a given visitor will have a system able to use the full range of the whiteboard's capabilities. So how and when and where do the several systems involved discover and hook up the capabilities they share?

- **Dawn arrives, bringing her "Virtual Monopoly" set, which uses the new Zapp-O Virtual Dice, certified by VeriPlay (an independent testing organization) to produce a statistically random "roll."**
  A different kind of external reference here: a re-usable, in fact portable, object guaranteed by a third party to fulfill a certain specification. Other examples suggest themselves: a deck of cards certified to shuffle thoroughly and always deal from the top; a cash register which guarantees secure and anonymous transactions. How do we provide for functionality which overrides or enhances or constrains what is pre-defined in the scene (e.g. locking a door, or making a wall transparent)?

- **Dawn's game has two different modes of play: in addition to the familiar board-and-pieces mode, which prevents players from moving out of turn and always moves them the right number of steps in the right direction** [Remember, the dice, the counters and the game were all developed independently], **there is also an "immersive" mode, in which the players shrink down so that the houses and hotels on the board seem life-size.**
  How does the browser know how much to shrink the avatars, and how to adjust their location and speed of motion? Alternatively, if the "shrinkage" is simply realized by transporting the players into a different scene, how are the actions in that scene replicated on the board in Art's living room?

- **Two days after the memorable Monopoly game, Art discovers that the dogbot has left him a gift: a lumpy brown object behind the sofa.** Note: Chuck's avatar brought the dogbot into the scene; this imported object then created a new object which remained in the scene after its (uninvited and unmanaged) creator left. **When clicked, the brown heap turns out to be—not what you thought, but a puppy, which runs around like mad and leaves bright yellow stains on the furniture.**
  If this is beginning to sound like a virus, then our point is made. Multi-user virtual worlds, like any shared application, will require a full range of reliable mechanisms for protecting their content from inappropriate access and manipulation.

This scenario exposes the complexity of the "distribution" that must be managed to make immersive social applications possible. Virtual online communities will not be designed by single authors, they will not be constructed entirely in any one language, and they will not be under any one operator's control. Rather, they will have to support continual negotiations among objects created without any knowledge of each other, some of which will be "driven" (at times) by unpredictable humans, and the effects of multiple, independently authored, more or less arbitrarily interacting application programs.

Robert Rockwell, PhD (1947–1998)

978-0-595-47390-8
0-595-47390-3

Printed in the United States
101400LV00006B/49/A